P9-APL-152

DIARY
OF A VOID

DIARY
OF A VOID

A NOVEL

Emi Yagi

TRANSLATED FROM THE JAPANESE BY
DAVID BOYD AND LUCY NORTH

VIKING

VIKING
An imprint of Penguin Random House LLC
penguinrandomhouse.com

Originally published in Japan as 『空芯手帳』(*Kūshin techō*) by
Chikumashobo Ltd., Tokyo, in 2020
First English-language edition published in North America by Viking, 2022

LIBRARY OF CONGRESS CATALOGING-IN-PUBLICATION DATA

Names: Yagi, Emi, 1988– author. | Boyd, David (David G.), translator. |
North, Lucy, translator.
Title: Diary of a void / Emi Yagi ; translated from the Japanese by
David Boyd and Lucy North.
Other titles: Kūshin techō. English
Identifiers: LCCN 2021057687 (print) | LCCN 2021057688 (ebook) |
ISBN 9780143136873 (hardcover) | ISBN 9780525508366 (ebook)
Subjects: LCGFT: Novels.
Classification: LCC PL877.5.A346 K8713 2022 (print) |
LCC PL877.5.A346 (ebook) | DDC 895.63/6—dc23/eng/20220304
LC record available at https://lccn.loc.gov/2021057687
LC ebook record available at https://lccn.loc.gov/2021057688

Printed in the United States of America
1st Printing

BOOK DESIGN BY LUCIA BERNARD

Translators' note: The Japanese title for this book, *Kūshin techō*, echoes that of *Boshi techō*, or the *Maternal and Child Health Handbook*, a booklet issued by Japan's Ministry of Health, Labor, and Welfare to all expectant mothers to enable them to chronicle their pregnancy, the health and development of the baby, and the details of their child's medical visits (vaccinations, dental checkups, etc.) up until age seven. In the novel's title, *kūshin* replaces "mother and child" with an "empty core" or, in our translation, a "void."

DIARY
OF A VOID

WEEK 5

The evening vegetables looked so fresh and juicy, the tips of the greens bursting with life. Nothing like the vegetables I'd find on my usual nighttime visits. And the shoppers, too, looked different, still so full of energy. I could see it in their faces. They were all about to go home with their purchases, cook themselves dinner, and settle down for the evening with full bellies.

Was this even the same supermarket? Where were the packs of wrapped sashimi beginning to dry up, the slabs of chicken steeped in puddles of pink water? Where were the shoppers bitterly eyeing the few remaining products, drawn only by the end-of-day sales? At this moment, the store seemed intent on making sure we knew this was its busiest time of day. The lights on the ceiling shone brightly over an immaculate, sparkling white floor, the eternally looping store jingle playing just loud enough for the name of the chain to worm itself into customers' ears.

I chose the shortest line and waited to check out. In front of me was a short man, his head barely up to my shoulder, his back bent with age. In his basket, obviously a weight on his flabby but hardly fat arms, I saw a family-sized pack of kurobuta pork. Product of Kagoshima. Must be shabu-shabu night.

I got back to my apartment, carrying my own bulging bag of food. As I pushed open the door and stepped into the darkness, I felt light-headed. I kicked off my heels and sank down right where I was. For a while I just lay there on the imitation wood floor, giving myself over to the familiar coolness, relieved to be out of the oppressive heat. Late summer was still dragging on—I was bored with being bored with it. When I lifted my head, I saw the sun still shining through at the other end of the room. A vision of paradise.

So this is pregnancy. What luxury. What loneliness.

I got pregnant four days ago.

"Huh? The cups are still . . ." my section head muttered as he returned to his desk. The smell of tobacco mixed with the stale evening air. He kept going.

2

"When was that? Oh yeah, the meeting we had after lunch."

He said the last part a bit louder. He can say it as loud as he wants. It's not like they're gonna get up and walk themselves to the sink.

Nobody looked up. And why should they? He wasn't talking to them. I, too, lowered my gaze. I kept my eyes on my computer, staring at one spot on the screen. The flat gray disintegrated into a pattern of lines. I'm busy. I really am. I have a deadline to meet. And I have to finish my report for the first half of the year. Just like everybody else.

A shadow appeared over the spreadsheet on my screen.

"Hey . . . Cups?"

He's talking to the cups now. So weird. With my mouth shut to keep out his hot, dry breath, I just banged on the space bar over and over.

"Shibata."

The section head was right behind me. I felt like I could see the cigarette smoke.

"Shibata, the coffee cups are still out. The cups in the meeting room."

Oh. Okay.

As I slowly stood up, he returned to his chair at

the far end of the line of desks. He adjusted the orthopedic seat cushion he'd bought online and sat down.

Everyone kept their heads down. Of course they did. The dirty cups weren't their responsibility. I bet the cups had never even crossed their minds. I picked up a trash can that lay on its side in the middle of the walkway, then made my way to the meeting room.

What we called "the meeting room" was nothing more than a space equipped with a few small tables and chairs. The partitions that set it off had scraps of transparent tape stuck all over them. How did they get there? What purpose did they serve? I had no idea, but every screen on the floor was the same, covered in countless sticky bits of tape. There was a conference room downstairs, but it didn't get much use. It was reserved for department managers and above.

What I did wasn't supposed to be an act of rebellion—more like a little experiment. I was curious. I wanted to see if it even occurred to any of my coworkers, maybe somebody who'd actually been in the meeting, to clean up. "Geez, what a long meeting, I thought it was never gonna end. Oh—the coffee cups. We can't just leave them like that, right? It's too much to ask Shibata to do it. I mean, she's the one who made the coffee for us and brought it over."

I think I just wanted to know what would happen if nobody was there to keep an eye out, to rush over as soon as the meeting ended and deal with the messes they'd made.

And I still might have obliged had I not been met with the sight of dirty cups, some still with coffee in them, and stuffed with cigarette butts. The odor of old cigarettes left sitting there for hours—it was now four thirty in the afternoon—was too much for me.

"Excuse me!" I said as my section head walked by, no doubt on his way to the break room. He had his mug and a tea bag. Lately he'd been obsessed with medicinal tea.

"Do you think you could take care of the cups today?"

"Huh?"

"I can't do it."

"Why? What's going on?"

"I'm pregnant. The smell of coffee . . . it triggers my morning sickness. The cigarettes, too . . . Anyway, isn't this supposed to be a nonsmoking building?"

And that's how I became pregnant.

When HR asked when the baby was due, I said the first date that came to mind: the middle of May.

Which meant, working backward, I had to be five weeks in. A little early to share the big news, I know.

HR advised me to consult my coworkers about whether any adjustments should be made to my work schedule. I went to see my section head. He went to see the department manager. The department manager didn't know what to do. And why should he? I was the only woman in my section. There'd been two other women before me, but one quit to look after her elderly parents, the other left when she got married.

On the off chance that they'd agree, I requested that I be allowed to leave work at five—for the time being, just until I got over the worst of my morning sickness. To my surprise, they said yes. No questions asked. Who knew what had been said behind my back—but if they couldn't say it to my face . . . I was going to be able to cut down on my workload and leave the office two or three hours early. Neither the section head nor the department manager seemed to have any detailed memory of his wife's pregnancy, and that had worked in my favor.

What seemed of greatest concern to my bosses, rather than when I could clock out, was the question of the coffee. Who would make it? Who was going to deal with the cups? Where was the milk? They asked me to type up step-by-step instructions. One day, when I wasn't around, they had a meeting in which it was decided that a young guy who'd started right out of college two years ago would be in charge of the coffee.

"Hey, this isn't so bad!" he exclaimed as I showed him what to do. You're right about that, I said back. That's why it's called instant coffee.

———○————————○———

At first I figured there must be some kind of concert or game that everyone was taking the train to. That, or the entire car was packed with people returning to the office after an on-site meeting. For a train to be this crowded this early with people simply going home was unreal. And these people didn't look particularly pleased either. It was as if going home at 5:00 p.m. was the most natural thing in the world. I was truly amazed.

The passengers seemed to be of two kinds: men and women in their fifties and sixties or women in their twenties. The latter were staring at their phones, holding them in one hand while resting the other on their soft, glamorous-looking dresses and skirts. Many of these women were made up beautifully, not like the women I found traveling with me when I usually got the train home. These young women had no experience of their makeup letting them down at any hour of the day, let alone late at night. The orange on their cheeks glowed, as if they'd brushed it on just moments ago.

The women in their fifties and sixties had no makeup on. Nearly all of them were wearing long-sleeved tops. Not dress shirts, not blouses, not sweaters, but pretty much T-shirts—just the simplest, most basic garment you could imagine. Quite a few of them were wearing white or black, but looking farther up the train car, I could see pastels: light pink, yellow, purple. Evidently these tops were worn with loose pants and sneakers. I stood there watching as the woman standing across from me in a light green top coolly took out her thermos, poured herself a cup of tea, and drank it. I thought I could hear ice clinking around inside the thermos.

I got off the train and dropped by the supermarket. One by one I selected the meat and vegetables I needed, following the recipe I'd found online while on the train. There's so much food to choose from at this time of day. Fresh vegetables, fresh fish in season, all at such low prices . . . Into my basket they went. While waiting to check out, I glanced outside. Some boys in high school uniforms were hanging around a takoyaki stall, all carrying sports bags with the same school name printed in big letters. The boys blew on the steaming takoyaki before cramming the balls into their mouths. They were all so tan. They looked practically identical.

My shopping done, I got back to my apartment, amazed by the fact that it was only six thirty. When I stepped out onto the balcony, I heard a piano. Someone was practicing one phrase, repeating the same thing over and over. I gathered the laundry I'd hung out to dry, folded it, put it away, gave the room a quick vacuum, and then started making my dinner: root vegetables and chicken. With that simmering on the stove, I made miso soup and a salad. I put eggplant in the soup. The salad was greens and chikuwa steeped in dashi. Now that I had the time for it, I could make sure to eat well—the sort of meal that a pregnant woman deserved. My skin was looking great. Maybe I'd gained a little weight.

The day before, during lunch, the guy who sat opposite me asked, "How are you feeling? How's your morning sickness?"

"Not bad. It's been pretty mild . . ."

"Glad to hear it. And you've given up your usual

premade lunches. When a woman's pregnant, she's got to do her very best to take care of herself."

For about a week, I'd been making my own lunches.

A s I finished eating my dinner, night fell at last, and a breeze started to blow in through the screen, wafting over my legs. I got up to close the curtains, pressing the button for the bath on my way over.

With my newfound free time, rather than taking rushed showers, I was enjoying long soaks in the tub. Occasionally I'd use bath products I'd received as party favors at weddings. Up until now I'd simply left them unopened under the bathroom sink. Maybe it was all in my head, but these high-quality products were great for relieving my fatigue. Come to think of it, I could have made much better use of them when things had been really busy at work—those times when I wouldn't get back home until close to midnight and would be too exhausted to speak. Strange how when you're totally drained, a bubble bath tends to be the last thing on your mind.

Today I took a bath in some Dead Sea salts. My tub was transformed into one of the saltiest bodies of water on earth. The salts were apparently going to enter my sweat glands, stimulating me to perspire, getting rid of my impurities. I leaned back in the hot water. Was I imagining things, or was I actually floating? Lying there, utterly naked in the Dead Sea, I remembered a dugong I'd seen years ago at the aquarium. Floating there in the dark green water. The picture of innocence, as if it had never once been involved in any weird plans—its own, or anyone else's.

Maybe it was the bath salts. When I got out and blow-dried my hair, I felt a little hot. I could hear the voices of neighborhood children. I positioned the electric fan in the middle of the room (I still hadn't gotten around to packing it away), turned it on, and lay down on my armchair. I didn't put on any music.

I've always thought of myself as a big music fan. When I walk to the station, or when I'm waiting for a friend or a train, I listen to music on my phone. I go to festivals and shows every summer. But listening to music alone in my room, with all the time in the world . . . I wouldn't know what to do with myself. An artist, someone I couldn't see, singing, putting their heart and soul into it. Where should I look, what kind of face should I make? The more members in the band, the more awkward I felt. What did other people do—people who thought of themselves as music lovers? Did they just sit there with their eyes closed as they took it in? Did they stare off, bobbing their heads and moving along to the music? Here I was, more than thirty years of life behind me, still completely unaware of the simplest things.

I turned off the light and curled up on the armchair, making a pillow out of the armrest. I tried singing something out loud, as if I were testing out a pen on the white space of the ceiling. My singing voice sounded high and a little breathy. But it wasn't bad. I got into it and kept going for a while. When I looked over at the clock, I saw that it was about the time I usually started eating dinner.

The night was still young.

For about a week I'd been doing stretches before go-ing to bed. A woman who worked in another section had come over to my desk and told me I ought to start getting fit early on in pregnancy. To make sure I was ready for what was to come.

She gave me some pages that had to be photocopies from a magazine from another decade. The eyebrows of the model doing the exercises were anachronisti-cally thin, her dress sheer and lacy. I don't know why, but the image of the doctor was blurry even though everything else was clear. With nothing better to do, I decided to try out one or two of the moves. They really did ease the tightness in my neck and shoulders, so I decided to keep them up.

Along with the exercises, the woman gave me some herbal tea, roasted in some special way by a gymnas-tics teacher friend of hers. Apparently it had lots of folic acid in it. It was an intense yellow color, and had a sort of sulfurous smell, but I started to drink it and found that I liked it. Today I was drinking it cold and diluted. Down it went. Down into the void that was my belly.

Apart from that woman, the others in my section, and the person I spoke to in HR, nobody else asked about my pregnancy. Not to my face, at least. The section head announced it to everyone in the production management unit meeting at the end of the month. I'd be taking maternity leave in the spring, he said. Beginning in January, my work would gradually be given to others. Once my pregnancy was officially announced, the men in my section made a point of treating me with deference. If we bumped into each other by our desks, they'd let me pass. Every time I took a break, they'd ask if I was okay. But they said nothing else. No "Congrats!," no "Is it a boy or a girl?" I could only assume that was because I wasn't married.

Whether or not that was the case, it did seem that most of the people at the paper core manufacturer where I worked now knew . . . just like that woman who brought me the tea. From time to time I noticed my belly being eyed: when I was in the elevator, when

I was using the copier. A few days before, I'd entered the cafeteria to get something to drink, and the room fell silent. Whatever it was that people had been discussing was just dropped, and all that remained were awkward and uncomfortable faces. In moments like that, I'd just put my hand on my empty belly and give it a little pat. I could at least act the part. It's all about how you carry yourself.

The only person who ever seemed to want to talk to me, and quite insistently, was Higashinakano. At the end of one meeting, he stopped me as I was walking back to my desk.

"Have you decided on a name?"

Well, I don't know yet if it's a boy or a girl, I told him. Oh, that's right, he said as he started counting off on his fingers. Then, apparently convinced, he nodded a few times and hurried off. With every nod, tiny white flakes fell from his head. It had to be dandruff.

After that, he started asking me several times a day how I was feeling. His desk was next to mine, so all I had to do was throw a cardigan over my shoulders and he'd ask if I'd caught a chill. If I coughed, he'd tell me to go to the hospital and get checked out. One day, he was taken to task by the section head for some problem in a report of his, so he ran to his keyboard and started tapping away—presumably to fix the issue as soon as he could. But before long, he said "Shibata," then passed me a slip of paper. At the top, it said "What You Should Eat When Pregnant, and What You Should Absolutely Avoid." Next to hijiki it said, "OK to eat this, but never more than twice a week," in ominously large letters.

Higashinakano always smelled like glue. The stuff I used when I was a kid. It wasn't a bad smell or anything, but it wasn't good, either. It was just the smell of glue. The funny thing is, I'd been sitting next to him for over a year, but I'd never actually seen him use glue—not even once.

WEEK 10

Over the weekend, I went out for drinks with a couple of friends at a basement izakaya near Hibiya. Two women, former coworkers who had joined my old company the same time I did.

Near where we were sitting, on the other side of a thin divider, was a group of men who had to be around my dad's age. Their conversation found its way over to us, along with thick clouds of cigarette smoke. We had no choice but to listen to their stories about their good old school days, all the wining and dining they did back in the bubble era, the parking lot business that one of them had recently started. We tried to have a conversation of our own, about health and beauty and everything in between. Momoi was telling us about the Chinese herbal remedies she was trying out to alleviate the headaches and moods she was getting after her period.

"Yeah, tell me about it," Yukino said. "The other night, I went out with my husband . . ."

With Yukino, when she says "Tell me about it," it pretty much always means that she isn't listening to what anyone else is saying. I bit into a chunk of boiled octopus. It was still weirdly cold. It had to have been frozen.

"He got tickets to one of those art aquariums from a client and he asked me if I wanted to go. It was pretty. But there were two college kids right in front of us, boyfriend and girlfriend. And the guy was telling the girl he'd stick by her side, no matter what. Even if the whole world turned against her. I mean . . . come on . . . right?"

"Some people really say stuff like that," Momoi chimed in, scanning the list of drinks. Maybe because the place was so dim, she had the menu right up to her face. A few short strands of stiff-looking hair fell forward from behind her ears. Come to think of it, I hadn't seen her with long hair since she'd had her first child.

"No, that's true, but . . ." Yukino began.

"What?"

"Well, why do you want to turn the whole world

against your girlfriend like that? I mean, when was the last time the whole world turned against anybody? Good luck taking on the whole world anyway. . . . Like, if he really loves her, shouldn't he just stop her before she does anything stupid enough to piss off the whole world?" Yukino said, then took a sip of her drink. It looked like some sort of cocktail with a big ball of ice cream on top. Tiny bubbles were floating up from under the ice cream. A highball float? Does that even exist? I wanted to see if I could find it on the menu, but Momoi was still flicking through it with a frown on her face.

Yukino was always quick on the uptake. Way ahead of everybody else. She was the first in our cohort to leave the company, and the first to get married. A few years earlier, we'd gone on a girls' trip to a hot spring and I noticed that her eyeliner remained beautifully thick even after she'd removed her makeup, so I asked her about it. She said that she'd had her lash line tattooed on. "You wouldn't believe the agony." And she went on to describe it, making Momoi and me wince in pain.

"But you and your husband get along great, don't you? How long have you guys been together now?"

Momoi asked. Apparently unable to make any sense of the menu, she called the waiter over and asked for another draft beer.

"Seven, eight years? I don't know that I'd call our relationship 'great.' But it's just the two of us, so it's easy enough. . . ."

"Hey, that's something. Your husband runs his own business, right? I think I saw an interview with him somewhere, maybe online."

"Well, it's good when business is good. But it's not always good for the family. Hey, speak of the devil . . . I gotta take this. He's always calling me over the smallest things, I swear."

As Yukino got up with her phone in her hand, Momoi and I took a moment to check our own phones. "Crap. . . . I completely forgot," Momoi said. Her kids and some friends were having a picnic the next day.

"I haven't thought at all about the food. . . . I can't keep giving them nothing but precooked stuff—not this time. I should probably stop by the supermarket on the way home. . . ."

"Picnic. Haven't heard that word in a while. No rest, huh?"

"Well, at least I get along with the other moms.

Not like the ones at the nursery school. You wouldn't believe the comments I get about the kids' lunches on sports day. Those moms are real monsters. . . ."

Yukino came back once her call was over, and suddenly it felt like things were about to wrap up. Momoi gulped down the beer that had only just been brought to the table, barely stopping to breathe, then asked the waiter for the bill.

We left the izakaya, emerging to find the street packed with people checking out the shop windows and college students gathering to go drinking with friends. Yukino and Momoi were going to the JR station at Yurakucho, and I needed to get the subway from Hibiya. We went our separate ways. As I stood in front of the subway ticket gate, searching my bag for my Suica pass, I caught sight of the little gifts I'd meant to give them from my visit back home over the summer. It was a little after nine on a Saturday night. The subway was empty.

I got off at the station closest to home. Something was missing, but I wasn't sure what. I wasn't hungry. I decided to drop by a bookstore. A woman my age stood in front of the racks, her face deep in a magazine. It was one of those magazines for pregnant women. Every now and then, she adjusted the pastel-pink handbag she'd hooked over her arm. Then I noticed something dangling from the handle. Hm . . . come to think of it . . . I took out my phone, did a quick search, then headed straight back into the station.

In a matter of minutes, I'd obtained my own maternity badge. All it took was a visit to the station office.

"Congratulations," the woman at the counter said. "Here it is."

"Actually, can I have two? While I'm here . . ."

I wanted one for my tote bag, for when I went to work, and another for my backpack, which I took with me when I had a lot to carry. The last time I'd attached anything to my bag had been just before college exams—that good luck charm from Yushima Shrine that my grandma had apparently gone out of her way to buy for me.

WEEK 11

The first person to notice the maternity badge on the strap of my bag was, of course, Higashinakano. The minute I appeared on Monday morning, he stopped his habitual leg shaking and locked his eyes on the little image of mother and child.

"You're finally getting into the spirit."

I gave a noncommittal nod.

"I bet you're going to have a boy, Shibata.... I just have a feeling...."

Oh yeah? I was about to say. What makes you so sure? But a call came in on the internal line, and he took it. I had no idea what was going on, but he just started apologizing, over and over, in that ridiculously loud voice of his. Higashinakano seemed to have to apologize to somebody almost every day.

As a result of my new badge, people started getting up and giving me their seats on the train. No, please, I don't need it, I'd say. But they'd insist, so I'd end up playing along. Part of me wanted to lift my blouse and show them my belly so they could see I really didn't need it. But I decided against it. That would just make things awkward.

Something . . . almost imperceptibly . . . seeped out of me. Oh. That explains the weird chills I'd had all morning. I quietly congratulated myself for wearing a black skirt to work today. I'd almost gone for my white chinos. Reaching for the little pouch in my bag, I looked around, then slipped it into my pocket so nobody saw. After all, this wasn't supposed to be happening to me.

I made my way quickly along the hallway, which was now completely empty of people. But the voices coming from the ladies' bathroom stopped me at the door. This was the time when women from other sections who hadn't finished getting ready at home did their makeup in front of the bathroom mirrors. Mondays and Fridays were especially bad. Ordinarily I wouldn't have cared, but this was different. The toilets in this building didn't have those devices that are supposed to mask bathroom sounds. If I tore a pad out of its wrapping, everybody would hear it. I didn't want anybody thinking I'd had a miscarriage or an abnormal bleed. Or do pregnant women use pads anyway, when . . . ? I should have looked into that.

As I wondered how I was going to pull this off, I felt something falling inside me. A warm, soft mass. Something like the innards of a dissected bird . . . A vision of the chicken liver I'd eaten last week flickering before my eyes, I headed straight for the elevator.

I didn't think I was doing that bad. Not at all— especially for someone who was losing blood at that moment. The first floor had a travel agency with bathrooms for staff and customers. No one looked twice when I walked in. Some good thinking there.

When I emerged from the stall, a commercial advertising a trip to Hawaii was playing. I took my time washing my hands. The building's sinks had hot water, and the toilet seats were warmed throughout the year, except in the middle of summer, and that almost made up for the absence of sound-masking devices. When I was done washing my hands, I took one of the pills out of my pouch and swallowed it. I always needed a painkiller on the first day. But I wondered if these pills were off-limits to someone who was pregnant. Better not take one at my desk, lest Higashinakano see me. Then I'd be in real hot water.

Visit Rome, Florence, and Venice on an eight-day trip starting from just one hundred ninety thousand yen! For details, talk to one of our representatives, or pick up a pamphlet at the front of the store!

At this moment, when my body felt at its worst, why did I have to listen to insufferable ads like this? I hung my ID card around my neck. No Rome for me. I wasn't going anywhere but back to my desk. My cramps were so bad I could barely walk. My hands and feet almost numb with cold.

"Shibata, everything okay? You aren't looking so good. I've got some painkillers in my desk. Bufferin. Loxonin . . . But maybe you should just try to tough it out, since, well . . ."

Higashinakano scrambled around, looking for something in his drawer. I couldn't take my eyes off the big brown stain on his sleeve. It almost looked like a mole—a really fat one. I gripped the bulging pouch in my hand.

"It's okay. It's nothing."

I still had cramps when I got home. I turned up the temperature for my bath and, while I waited for the tub to fill, I tallied up my expenses for the month. I'd been using an app on my phone to keep track of everything, but my credit card payments were a little too complicated, so I'd gone back to using Excel on my computer.

Apparently I'd spent a little more than I had intended to. One by one I checked off items. Trips, zero. Clothes, zero. Eating out . . . Since getting pregnant, I was bringing my lunch to the office. . . . Hm. What about medical expenses? They did seem way higher than last month.

Right. I remembered the notice that had come in the mail telling me that the annual payment for my insurance was going to be withdrawn from my account. I'd enrolled in a plan just before my thirtieth birthday, at the urging of my mom, who insisted that the earlier you joined, the more you got for your money. Fortunately, I'd never had any major health problems. I'd always been perfectly healthy, without even trying to be.

One other row had shot up, too: hobbies and interests. This was no surprise—I'd gone to a music festival and it set me back more than I thought it would. The plan had been to go with Momoi, but her youngest had come down with a fever, so I ended up going by myself. Momoi had offered to pay her half of the rental for the tent, but hearing her screaming kid on the other end of the line, I couldn't bring myself to make her pay and wound up paying for it all. Anyway, it was a good weekend.

Oh well. No point in changing my insurance policy now, and it's not like I go to music festivals all the time. But what about the renewal fee for my apartment? That was coming up in January. I had some money set aside, but I had to be careful. I hadn't been working overtime since getting pregnant. I was going to have to save up somehow. I had to make it through maternity leave.

I glanced at a folder that I'd kept at the end of my bookshelf. A couple of months ago, my mom had sent me a box of things—a bag of rice, some apples, a plastic avocado slicer from her favorite hundred-yen store, and this folder. Opening it up, I saw printouts for condos and apartments for sale in the city, and schemes for loans and mortgages. She must have found all this stuff online, I thought. I should throw it out. But then a large Post-it caught my eye. It had figures written on it, showing monthly payments on a mortgage for a small one-bedroom apartment downtown. Below that was a message, clearly written by my dad. It was his handwriting, every character looking like a skinny fish. "Give it some thought. We can help a little with the money."

I looked away. A truck passed by on the road outside. My window rattled.

I shut my laptop and began my exercises. The stretches involved getting on my knees and elbows, so I did them on my kilim rug—the brick-red kilim that I'd bought years ago on a trip to Turkey.

That was six years ago, when I'd just moved to this apartment. For six years, I'd been eating my breakfast here, making myself up here every morning. . . . So many days and nights now gone, never to return, with nothing to remember them by. The steam that rose as I cooked a late dinner for myself, my favorite mascara . . . They'd vanished without a trace, without a sound, as if they'd never been there at all.

After my stretches, I lay down on the rug. For some reason, the outline of the things around my room suddenly seemed so clear. The tiny armchair I'd brought from home, the low table I liked to eat at, the vase on the windowsill, the cosmos inside it. The silhouette of each of these things seemed extraordinarily dark. In that darkness, I got the distinct impression that these all-too-familiar objects were looking at me, sizing me up. I got back on my laptop, splaying my fingers over the pattern of my kilim as I got up.

As I opened up an application form for a mutual fund, the words "Investment Objective" appeared on the screen. After reviewing all the options, I decided to go with "Child's Education." As I clicked the words, a melody rang out, letting me know that the bath was ready. The song was "Home on the Range."

WEEK 14

○——————————————○

I knew I should have gotten out of bed earlier. I struggled to get my feet into my shoes. Ten more minutes and I wouldn't have had to rush. Finally I got my Converse All Stars on. It was great that I could wear sneakers to work, but I still had more than six months to go. Could I really make it?

In the glass door downstairs, I saw my own reflection: just a woman in a pair of white sneakers. Still no hint of a baby bump.

"Shibata. Are you still okay coming to work?" Higashinakano sidled up behind me. I was busily putting away the tables that had been brought out for the meeting.

"Yeah. I can handle it."

"How many weeks in are you?"

"About three months? Hey, since you're there, can you push the table this way just a bit?"

"This one?"

"The one next to that."

"Got it, got it."

The people who'd been helping out were all heading back to their desks. Maybe they figured it was fine to leave the rest to me, or maybe they saw it was time for lunch? Irritated, I clicked my tongue—softly, so Higashinakano wouldn't hear.

Out the meeting room window, the sky looked so clear and blue it was dizzying. The gingkos were starting to form their usual golden ridges. Once noon rolled around, there were always lots of people walking outside, clutching their purses and wallets. In front of the office was the usual food truck, with loads of people lined up. Come to think of it, I hadn't bought anything from them in a while—not since I got pregnant.

"Shibata," Higashinakano called out behind me as he lined up the chairs. "Seriously, you shouldn't be doing this. There are other people who can put the tables away. Okay, I know everyone runs off as soon as it's time for lunch, but . . . soon your belly's going to start showing. . . ."

Higashinakano pointed awkwardly at his own belly, then left the room. I stared at my reflection in the window. Damn. Looking at my flat stomach, I clicked my tongue again. This time there was no one to hear me.

The night before, after my bath, I looked up the stages of pregnancy online. Amid sites run by medical experts and blogs run by expectant mothers, some pregnancy tracker apps came up. Most of them were supposed to help pregnant women monitor their moods and keep track of things like diet, but some offered a lot of information about the stages of pregnancy and the changes that could be expected in the fetus. I downloaded one. I figured I might as well. Baby-N-Me. It turned out to be run by a diaper company. I found the frequent popups and banners offering thirty lucky moms-to-be the chance to win a year's worth of diapers irritating, but the simple design appealed to me, and the pictures of the fetus they had were really cute.

The explanations of changes in the mother's body and the fetus were divided up into weeks, starting from right after conception. Let's see, I was now in my fourteenth week. This meant I was past the stage when morning sickness was the most unbearable, and when I was most at risk of miscarriage. Good to know.

Looking at the weeks just before and after where I was, I saw week twelve was the one in which my belly would start to show, just a little. This was also when women started to put on weight—their appetite would return as their morning sickness waned. At week fourteen, the fetus measures around nine centimeters from head to butt and weighs just about 1.5 ounces. Right now, the app told me my baby was the size of a small plum. This app apparently put the size of the baby in terms of a different fruit each week. At week thirteen, an apricot. At week fifteen, a grapefruit.

So it was about time for my belly to start showing a little. Higashinakano was right. A quick search online turned up fake baby bumps, like the kind that actresses use when they play expectant mothers. For some reason, though, I couldn't find any to buy. I checked Amazon and Mercari, but got nowhere. Anyway, that would be for much later on—nothing I'd need anytime soon.

Instead, I grabbed a bunch of hand towels and socks and, standing sideways in front of my full-length mirror, stuffed them inside my clothes. This was going to be trickier than I thought. To get the size right. And to make it look natural. Well, clearly, hand towels were useless. Too flat if you folded them, too bulky if you balled them up. Plus, under dresses they just fell out. The shape was totally off. Socks were similarly useless. They had no bulk.

Tights, though, actually did the trick. Perfect for molding into a soft, rounded form. The only thing was that they didn't have much volume. Thick winter tights were what I needed: probably at least 80 denier. This meant getting down my winter clothes from the loft. A glance at the clock told me it was already past midnight, and suddenly I couldn't be bothered. I could try on a few things in the morning as I got ready for work, I told myself, and crawled into bed.

But when morning came, I was way too rushed, and I had to go to work with a belly that was as flat as a board.

On my way to work, while wondering whether I was going to be crushed to death on the packed train, I thought about it some more. About junior high and high school students who couldn't tell their parents or teachers they were pregnant, and ended up giving birth in a bathroom stall . . . In fact, any number of the women on this train could be pregnant right now and not even know it.

But. I shouldn't forget. I had to think about Higashinakano, who had more time and attention to spare than the parent of a teenage daughter. Couldn't he just get married and have a baby of his own? That way I wouldn't have to be so self-conscious. That wasn't going to happen anytime soon. . . . Meanwhile, my due date was only getting closer. If I didn't do something fast, I could imagine him hauling me in to see an obstetrician. What could I do to get my belly bigger?

At lunchtime, Higashinakano set a colorful bandanna on his desk and unwrapped it to expose a bento box. It was plastic—the lunch box of a child. The contents pretty much never changed: a rice ball wrapped in limp nori, a spring roll or some fried chicken (no doubt frozen), a side of some green gunk that I never managed to figure out—it just looked like mud. Did he make lunch for himself? That weird rice ball disappearing slowly down his gullet while he made the most annoying sounds in the world. There was something about it that I couldn't stand.

Late in the afternoon, getting back from having been out of the office, I noticed a large cardboard box that had been left on my desk. On the delivery slip it said that the sender was one of our clients, a well-known purveyor of fruit desserts. The contents were listed as "Fruit Jelly." Peeking inside, I saw all these little cups in various colors: peach, orange, chartreuse. Gobs of peach and grapefruit napping peacefully in little cribs of gelatin.

There was a note attached: "Please enjoy!"

We often got gifts like this from our clients. And they always wound up on my desk. Some of the men were giving me glances, as if they were expecting something. Wait, that's exactly what they were doing. They were waiting for me to go desk to desk, handing out snacks and little spoons. "Some fruit cups came from one of our clients. . . . Do you want one?" I glanced up at the clock, shut the flaps of the box, and carried it into the break room.

My first task was to move the washcloth left between the sink and the draining board—the only bit of practical workspace. I never knew who put this washcloth here, but it was always here, as if this was where it actually belonged. It almost always smelled disgusting. Today, it smelled like it had been used to wipe up some milk. Plucking it up with the whites of my fingernails, I tossed it in the sink, then set the box down and started dismantling it. Each corner had been sealed with copious amounts of glue. When I tried to force it open, my nails bent back. I decided to use the box cutter I had in my pocket. Cutting-edge technology. I sliced into the box with the blade, and imagined stabbing every one of my coworkers.

The next step was to remove the paper and all the ribbons. The company's wrapping paper was covered in a cute, fruity pattern: I always hesitated before throwing out something like this, but I could never imagine what I might use it for. No, it wasn't worth keeping—it could go in the recycling. The ribbons, too. It was then that I noticed the state of the trash. Full would be an understatement. Stacks of paper so high that they were about to tip right over into the nonburnables. The receptacle for batteries was on its side. Quickly checking that no one was around, I tried shoving the wrapping paper between one tower of paper and the wall. At the slightest touch, the pile tipped over, covering the floor in copy paper and flyers.

I wanted to burst into tears. But really? Over a bunch of snack packs? I gritted my teeth and started picking up the paper. Halfway through, the head of another section came by with more paper to throw out. "That's really good of you, Shibata," he said, putting the trash directly into my hands, "making sure our break room stays nice and clean. . . ." I had a sudden urge to pick up one of the leaky batteries and fling it right at his skull.

Twenty minutes later, the cleanup behind me, the recyclable paper bound neatly with string, it hit me. If I had to give a jelly to each of my coworkers, I'd be three cups short. Well, I suppose I could go without one. Higashinakano, too. Now all I needed was for somebody to be out of office. Was anyone visiting clients today? But—wait a minute. Why was I so quick to deny myself this pleasure?

Just then, I felt something soft against my hand. A material that wasn't exactly paper, not exactly fabric, filling out the space in the box. It was oddly warm. I tried squishing it. Silently, it collapsed down to nothing, then, as I pulled my hand away, it slowly sprang back. Apparently designed to match the cups, it came in three bands of color: pink, orange, and chartreuse. Then I noticed bits of glitter, twinkling under the faint fluorescent break room light. I took it in both hands and drew it close. It swelled out slowly from within, like it was filling up with breath. I balled it up gently, wrapped it in my handkerchief, and headed for the bathroom.

I returned to my desk. A chartreuse jelly in one hand and a little spoon in the other. I put the rest of the jellies in the fridge, along with a note. "These are for everyone—in every department. Please help yourself!" I ripped the top off of my cup, thrust my spoon into the mirrorlike surface of the jelly, and scooped up a big chunk of grape. As I rolled the delectable fruit around in my mouth, several people who had been looking in my direction darted for the break room.

The little one under my blouse was grinning away, sparkling in three colors.

Another Monday, huh? Cold today, isn't it? I've never known how to reply when people greet you by stating the obvious. The best I can come up with is something equally vapid. Mondays, right? Yeah, it's practically freezing. . . .

So when the first thing Yukino said when we met up for a movie was "Shibata, you put on some serious weight," all I could say back was "Yeah, tell me about it." Any number of other possible responses rose in my throat. Yeah, now that my morning sickness is over . . . It's pretty normal when you're this far along. . . . But the words got stuck.

I'd been eating—a lot—since I downloaded that app.

Even before that, in fact, ever since I started getting home earlier and had the time to prepare three meals a day, I'd been eating better. But the moment I saw the words "second trimester" and the accompanying explanations—about how this is the time when morning sickness ends and things settle down—I felt strangely liberated. So I kept eating—as if my life depended on it.

In addition to my three balanced meals, I liked to pop into the convenience store before lunch, at around ten thirty, to get a doughnut, and in the afternoons I snacked on rice crackers while working. Worried about additives, Higashinakano pushed packets of crispy almonds and dried sardines on me. These would be healthier, he said. I finished them off as a quick snack between spreadsheets. A coworker who handled packaging for one of the major candy makers gave me a huge supply of Koala's March, which I also worked through in no time. As a child, I'd gotten such a thrill out of their cute expressions and striking poses, each one unique. Now I was tossing the bite-sized marsupials straight into my mouth. What was I turning into? It was terrifying.

That night, after my bath, I stood in front of the mirror. The woman looking back at me was distinctly pear-shaped. My face looked the way it always had. It was the bottom part of me that was different. I quickly dried myself off and tried on some skirts and jeans. Nothing looked right. My thighs were jutting out. And the way I looked from behind was . . . Well, it was just too painful to behold.

I grabbed a dress out of the closet and slipped it on. The only one I had. It was a summer dress that I'd bought on a trip to Bali that I took with Momoi before she got married. A riot of bright colors, it came down to my ankles. Clearly meant to be worn to the beach. No matter. It fit. But there was just one problem. It really accentuated my butt. Let me try stuffing the belly with a cotton stole to get the balance right. . . . Now look at that. In the mirror was the perfect image of a pregnant woman.

As I dried my hair, I looked online, found some other dresses that were more appropriate for work and bought them. Until they arrived, while everyone else was transitioning to winter, putting on coats and sweaters, I was going to stick with my summer dress and my usual work blazer. Dressed in the dazzling flowers of some tropical island adrift in an ocean of deep pink, there I sat, in a season and place all my own.

Once I started wearing dresses to work, I was now unmistakably pregnant. When I walked around the office, arms full of paper core samples, coworkers from other sections would come up and offer to carry them. When I was waiting for the elevator, they'd stay back and let me get in first. I even had an old woman, a complete stranger, volunteer a prediction. The baby, she said, would be arriving "next week." "Um, the due date is May," I said to her. "No, it's coming next week. Trust me, I can see it," she added before getting off the elevator, parting with one final detail: "And it'll be a healthy baby boy!"

Friday night. I followed my usual routine of stopping by the supermarket, then going home and cooking dinner. Flounder cooked in soy sauce, a dressed salad with pea sprouts and fried tofu, miso soup with lotus root and scallions, sautéed vegetables, and rice. After dinner, I did my stretches. The same woman who'd given me the exercises a few weeks back gave me another set, this time for early in the second trimester. Again, the image of the doctor playing the part of the instructor was blurry, and the model's thin, straight eyebrows reminded me of a bygone era. Still, these stretches were working wonders on my hips.

"Get your shoulders, hips, and knees in a straight line and count to ten."

Lifting my butt off the cold floor, I remembered what the woman who gave me the exercises had said.

"It probably doesn't feel real yet, but just think: you're bringing a new life into the world!" There was a touch of pride in her expression.

One . . . two . . . three . . . four . . .

Once I'd counted to ten, I headed into the kitchen. I took out the stubs of the pea sprouts I'd used in my salad, put them back in the plastic container, and watered them. I'd overfilled it, so I poured out a little water, set the container where it would get a lot of sun, and went back to my stretches.

The cropped pea sprouts made me think of how our dog looked after my mom tried to give him a trim. She'd been given that dog by an acquaintance, and she was positive he was a poodle, but he grew so big he broke the doghouse in the yard. Sometimes even my mom had to laugh about it.

WEEK 16

The day after a concert, work is always tough. Yesterday was especially hard on me. I'd gone to a big show just outside of the city, and afterward the buses were so crowded that it took me forever to get home. But even worse, the heat of it was still with me, in every part of my body—in my eyes, my ears, my chest. When I closed my eyes, I could see soft green lights squirming around in the darkness, fragments of sound would start to move, and the minute I tried to concentrate, I'd find myself back in that space. If I opened my mouth, I felt as though magical phrases—lines from the songs—would come pouring out of my throat. The gray jumper dress I'd bought online transformed into a shimmering silver costume in the spotlight.

I was yanked back to reality when a jumble of cardboard tubes was dumped on my desk. I was back in the overheated office, the smell of coffee hanging in the air.

I was at my job, on the fourth floor of this old office building.

I picked up the samples, examining them one at a time, replying to the questions coming at me from sales. These were to become wallpaper cores. It was an order for a new client, which was rare for us.

Paper cores were the last thing I ever thought I'd have a career in. My first job out of college was with a temp agency, which connected people who either wanted to find a new job or wanted to change jobs with companies that needed staff but didn't actually want to pay them a decent salary. I was there, but that was about it. I really couldn't see any point in what I was doing. All I did was have a phone call or two with the relevant people, call the candidates in, and fill out a bunch of forms. Form after form after form. It was endless. Please specify why the previous recruit was unsuitable. Please explain what you didn't like about your previous place of work. The only things that changed from one form to the next was the name of the recruit, the name of the company.

Yukino was the first of the three of us to leave the temp agency. This was just as we were about to enter our third year. Soon after that, it was Momoi's turn to be lured away. "If you're even thinking about it, you should move on," I told her. "This isn't the only company in the world." But for some reason I didn't take my own advice.

At twenty-five, I got promoted. One day I realized that nearly everyone who had joined with me had already left. A lot of older coworkers had retired. The people on my team, who weren't that much younger than I was, seemed to respect me, and I liked them well enough. But my promotion meant that I wouldn't get paid overtime. I still had to deal with the same number of clients; the only difference was that I had to attend more meetings and write more reports. I was now getting calls late at night from senior coworkers and clients on my private cell phone. I could no longer take vacations. I couldn't eat properly—I didn't have the time. I stopped getting my period.

One day I was contacted by a company that I'd supplied with a recruit. The guy I'd sent them apparently smelled bad, and they wanted me to give him a warning. He was in his late forties, thin as a rake, and he really did stink, as I discovered when we met. It wasn't just the smell of sweat. So I told him: you need to take baths.

After some time, the company contacted me again. The guy still stinks. Please, do something about it, right away. I met up with him again and told him he had to take a bath as soon as possible. "What—you wanna go to a hotel right now? You wanna give me a bath? Who the hell do you think you are?" He reached out and groped my breast. It was only a moment, I think, but his dirty, bitten-down fingernails seared themselves into my eyes. I told my boss what had happened over text, and thirty minutes later I got a response. "You should have said you'd go with him! Maybe I can join you guys?! (^_^)" This from a man in his fifties who was always trying to get me to meet up with him late at night, though the purpose of that "meeting" was never made clear to me. I didn't bother writing back. Instead I immediately opened up a job-search site on my phone and signed up.

In my interview with the agent, I stated my preference for a quiet environment, and said I'd do anything but sales. The agent pointed me to the job I have now. I hadn't been aware that paper core manufacturers even existed, and I had no idea what "production management" involved. The company's website, which I looked over before the job interview, was clearly a relic from another era, with patches of garbled text here and there. I found one page with the title "Best in the Industry! How We Learned to Make

Seamless Cardboard Tubes and Cores," emphasizing how difficult it was for them to discover the secrets necessary to actually produce "seamless" cores, not that anything I read meant anything to me.

But even in my ignorance, it seemed pretty obvious that smooth cylinders were better than rough ones. At any rate, this job seemed more worthwhile than thinking about how long it had been since some guy's last bath.

At the interview, two men—my section head and department manager—more or less gave me the job. "A woman college graduate! It'd be an honor. We actually had two women with us before. They were both part time, and we were sorry to see them go."

I got a real explanation of the job once I'd joined. I had to go over the details of orders that came in from sales, confirm them with clients, compile design instructions for the factory, and set up plans for the production line.

My first month here, I thought I was in heaven. No impossible quotas, no calls from clients waking me up in the middle of the night. It was fine to wear sneakers to the office and take a backpack in with me. No more blisters from having to run around in heels all day. I could go to concerts on weeknights.

Most of my coworkers had been with the company for years. This had been presented by the agent as one of the best things about the job. Almost nobody here raised their voice. It reminded me of the wetlands I visited with my family once when I was a child. So quiet and still, time just sliding slowly by.

Nevertheless, about a month and a half in, it hit me—as I was getting into the elevator, where the lights looked like they might peter out at any moment. My coworkers looked unwell. I'd had an inkling of this when I had shouted out my first greeting to everybody as a new recruit at the monthly meeting one morning, when the entire workforce assembled in one room. Everybody looked physically ill—like they were having liver problems. But, well, the building we were in was pretty dark—unlike my previous office, which had been on the twenty-second floor of a skyscraper. This one was old. It was probably the lighting. That's what I told myself.

But once I'd noticed it, I saw it everywhere. Eventually I figured it out. It was the long hours. The constant "meetings." For these meetings, pretty much everyone had to stop what they were doing, gather together, and listen while a senior coworker went on and on about the most random thoughts and gripes.

If you wanted to get a budget for a particular project approved, you had to put together a set of documents and get the department manager to sign off, produce a second set for the head of the section, a third for the president, then make color copies to pass out to the entire team. No thought was given to whether any of this served a purpose. There was neither time nor energy to object. Just do it. Don't ask questions. When the stress got to be too much, you simply got in the elevator, a pack of cigarettes in your shirt pocket, and went out for a smoke.

My work, however, involved a few additional tasks. They weren't named, and no one told me that they were mine. It was simply assumed.

At first I thought it was just temporary and it would stop when my job really started. Younger people would eventually be hired to handle the more menial tasks. As it was, I had to answer all incoming calls, make copies for anybody who asked, purchase supplies, sort the packages addressed to the different sections and distribute them, replace the paper and ink in the copy machines when they were running low, write the day's date on the office whiteboard, pick up any trash that had fallen on the floor, see to the paper shredders that had been left full, throw out the rotten food in the break room fridge, use rubbing alcohol to clean off the hardened chunks of chicken, egg, and rice that had exploded in the microwave. . . .

No one ever told me I had to do these things. But if I didn't take care of it, sooner or later there'd be a little comment.

"Hey . . . Microwave?"

My name's not Microwave.

One of my responsibilities was the coffee. When clients visited, I prepared the coffee and brought it over on a tray. It was instant coffee. Anybody could have done it. I frequently saw people making coffee for themselves. But the task seemed somehow beyond them when we had visitors. They'd just stare dolefully in my direction. If I kept doing my work, I'd hear:

"Hey . . . Coffee?"

Nope. That's not my name, either.

Some people seemed to think that making coffee involved meticulous event planning. Upon learning that I was going to be out of the office during a client's visit, they'd discuss it as if the fate of the world hung in the balance. "What are we going to do about the coffee in the afternoon meeting?" "No need to panic! I asked a girl from another section to help out." "You're a lifesaver!"

People seemed to be under the impression, at least in my section, that if they made coffee for somebody else, it would signify some deep personal inadequacy.

The only person who seemed not to get the memo was Higashinakano. I had learned that he'd once offered to take over coffee duties on a day the whole office was in a panic because I was out. But it didn't go well. He'd filled the cups to the brim, and a client had ended up with hot coffee all over his shirt. Higashinakano had been forbidden to serve the coffee ever again. How lucky for him, I thought. No one had ever suggested I even take a break from it.

The number of work projects coming my way grew and grew. Meanwhile, the other tasks, the unnamed ones, remained the same as ever. New recruits joined, young men straight out of college, and that occasionally meant a lessening of my official load, but the nameless tasks around the office remained my responsibility alone. Before I knew it, I was leaving the office late at night, when the pieces of sashimi at the supermarket near the station would be dry as fossils. Even the wet towels for customers in the bagging area were hard as rocks.

And the conversations with my coworkers. They didn't get off the ground. I couldn't connect with any of these people. One night, I was working overtime when the department manager stopped by my desk.

"Hey, cool band . . ." he said. He was pointing at one of the posters I had over my desk.

"What's cool about them?"

"Oh, they just look cool. . . . I dunno. . . ."

What kind of answer is that?

And yet, given the chance, he and all the other guys on the team were all too happy to make prying comments about my love life.

The office was a swamp. Not a deep one. But one that let off a weird-smelling gas all year round.

I was wondering whether I really wanted to continue to expose myself to the damaging effects of this swamp when they recommended that I join a group tour of the company's factory for new hires. The idea was to observe the manufacturing process, to gain a better understanding of what our company does. Someone in my role should have done this much earlier, but no one had had the time to show me around, so here I was.

The factory was about an hour's train ride from the office, out in the suburbs. It was a Monday. I'd gone to a show the night before—and I was still feeling a little out of it. My legs and arms felt weirdly cold, but my eyes and throat were on fire.

At the loading bay where the tour started, the rolls of paper that were about to be used in the process seemed stupidly big, like those cartoon character suits they wear at baseball games and theme parks. We walked by a smoking room with dark yellow walls. Halfway through the tour, they showed us a video about the factory. The sounds of the machines drowned out the narration, so most of it escaped me. When we finally passed through the heavy plastic curtains into the manufacturing area, paper dust danced in the harsh rays of the late afternoon sun. Our guide explained each piece of machinery as it lay there on the floor, as if utterly exhausted from all the work it'd had to do, and that was followed by a demonstration of paper cylinders being made, which we'd just managed to catch. By this time, several people in the group, drained from wandering through the dim space, weren't even bothering to hide their yawns.

Soon it would be over. The paper, which had been cut into long strips, was wound over a metal core and then chopped up into sections. That was it. There was no sophisticated technology, nothing to see. What came out were cylinders for plastic wrap, sticky tape, for more industrial items that you never even saw in the course of daily life. Ribbons of paper made their way through the equipment, running on and on. Heading straight for a metal core.

What was it all for? The machine had already come to a stop by the time I asked myself that question. The sound of the motor took a moment to fade, then all that was left was a batch of white cardboard tubes and some still-warm machinery. Nothing I couldn't have seen on video.

And that was the end of the tour. The last thing we had to do was submit a summary of our thoughts to HR within two days. There were still several hours before the end of the workday, but we were told we could go straight home. Some of the others said they were going out for drinks and asked me if I wanted to join, but I said no thanks and got on the train alone. On the ride back to the city, I was pretty much the only passenger. Leaning against a scuffed red seat, I recalled the sight of the cores as they came off the roller. The hypnotic movement of those ribbons moving forward, only to be wound round and round.

I wrote down some details that I had to confirm with the client before we could proceed with production, then handed my notes to the guy from sales. A new hire in his first year at the company. He gathered up all the samples and started loading them into a paper bag.

"Production Management," Higashinakano said loudly as he picked up the phone. He'd been banned from coffee duty, but he'd apparently been deemed worthy of handling calls.

WEEK 17

I was getting heavier. I now weighed nine pounds more than I did before I got pregnant. I decided I'd start walking. I'd get off the train one station before my usual stop, maybe two, and walk the rest of the way home. Today was my first day, so I decided I'd really commit. I got off two stations early.

When I exited the station, the shadows of evening were beginning to work their way into everything around me. The color of the sky was gradually becoming more intense: an ultramarine blue. The flowers in the planters in front of the drugstore seemed like white shapes floating in space.

I'd been riding this train line for years, but this was the first time I'd ever gotten off here. It wasn't a major hub, and I didn't see any tall buildings, but there had to be some schools and offices nearby. There was no end to the crowds of people. Most of them were heading into the station. Groups of students from middle school and high school and college, all with happy looks on their faces, people in dress shoes and pumps. The sun had gone down, and from a distance, the people around me just looked like dark figures. Only when we passed each other under the street-lamps could I make out their expressions. Walking along in the cold and dark, everyone looked so sure of themselves, as if they knew exactly what they should be doing—where they should be going—none of them lost, none of them bursting into tears because their fingertips were freezing. They all headed home quietly like battle-tested pros. A group of girls in matching track suits, probably on their way back from practice, were stuffing their faces with yaki-imo that looked nice and hot. I wanted some.

As I walked on, my route took me onto more resi-dential streets with overwhelmingly modest single-family homes and small, cheap apartment buildings. Apart from the houses, I saw cigarette stands and sake shops, all shuttered for the night, and a bunch of park-ing lots. There were fewer people around. Sometimes I'd see someone making their way along the road ahead. The next instant, they'd turn a corner and dis-appear. The soft footsteps I'd been hearing behind me would turn into the clang-clang-clang of iron stairs. Isn't that what people always did? Go their own way, never even bothering to let you know? One moment they're there, the next they're gone. And it all happens so quietly that you don't even realize they aren't there anymore.

I stopped to check the map on my phone. I saw a light go on in the window of the apartment right in front of me, then it went dark. The orange check curtains were quickly drawn tight, leaving only a faint glow in the window. I could hear a man and a woman talking, and the rustling of plastic bags.

The aroma of dried shiitake soup stock wafted out into the deserted streets. When I was a kid, I always hated that smell.

After walking through the neighborhood for a while, I emerged onto a road that I recognized. Two or three blocks ahead, I caught sight of something red floating in the darkness. The red was so vivid that I could see it clearly from a distance, even though the sun had already gone down. It drifted forward, stopped, then started moving slowly forward again. In the pale glow of the streetlamps and the faint light emanating from the windows of nearby houses, its movements were like that of a lost child.

I wondered if I should cut through to the next road. I'd heard about somebody getting their handbag snatched right around here about a week ago. The perpetrator still hadn't been caught. I'd seen a notice taped to a utility pole calling for witnesses.

If the victim lived on her own, the first thing she'd do would be to go to the police—the same as anybody. But once she'd done that, then what? What if somebody stole my bag? So much for my keys. The other people in my building were never going to buzz me in. I'd have to call the management company. But I wouldn't have my cell phone, so how was I supposed to get their number? Even if for some reason I had the number in my head, I'd have no cash on me, so I wouldn't be able to use a pay phone. Would someone at the police station help me through this? Anyway, at this time of night, they probably couldn't give me a new key until the next day. I'd have to spend the night at a hotel. And I'd have to pay for that. Damn. Just when I was trying my hardest to cut down on expenses . . . Wait up. I'm getting carried away, I tried telling myself. The next thing I knew, the red blur was right in front of me.

It was a person. A young woman. She was leaning against a telephone pole. Looking down, face turned slightly. She was beautiful. Night had fallen, and the air was cold. But the front of her bright red down jacket was unzipped all the way. Her big belly was popping out, rising and falling.

"Are you all right?" I asked. She looked up and adjusted her position a little. She had one hand up, hovering over her belly. The round belly under her sweater. She now held both hands over her belly, as if to shield it, and that was how she remained, slightly hunched over. Her long hair and her red jacket were trembling.

I tried talking to her again, this time a little slower. "Um, sorry . . . I don't mean to bother you, but. . . . I just wondered whether you're feeling okay. I have some water, if that'd help? I've already had some, but . . ."

She lifted her head. What a slender face! For a few seconds, her big black eyes locked onto mine. She looked frightened. The next moment her gaze traveled down, clearly taking in the maternity badge on my bag. BABY INSIDE. All at once, the tension left her shoulders.

"I'm okay." Her voice was like a xylophone, ringing out in a small room with nobody in it. "Really, I'm all right. Thanks."

She straightened right up, brushing the hem of her coat with one hand. She was taller than I expected. You sure you're okay? I wanted to ask, but she'd just told me she was, so I refrained.

We gave each other a slight bow, then walked away, heading in opposite directions. As I rounded the corner, I glanced back, trying to make it as natural a gesture as I could, and saw her slipping down some alley, her red coat disappearing beyond a concrete wall.

Taking out my phone, I checked my location. I was close to home.

As I went down the hill, I tried to conjure up a picture of the person I'd just encountered. I thought I'd taken in everything there was to see about her, but all I could recall was how slender her face was. Her belly was something else. It was so large, almost thrusting itself forward for me to touch it. There was no denying it—she was carrying the real thing, a real baby inside.

WEEK 18

I'd surprised myself. I had managed to keep walking pretty much every day. So this week I decided I'd try to walk over the weekend as well. Yesterday, Saturday, it was raining, so I didn't go out, but today the skies were clear and the sun was shining, and since I had nothing else to do, I set out a little earlier than I would during the week. The midafternoon streets were rendered clear and sharp under the gentle light of the sun, which would be setting soon. The trees on either side of the road, having stubbornly held on to their leaves well into December, maybe due to climate change, had looked absurdly red, but now they were completely bare.

My main intention was to explore my normal route in the light of day, and I'd start where I usually ended. As I made my way up the hill just past the local shrine, there, under the tangerine sun, I saw that same woman in the red down jacket. In the parking lot, leaning against a bulletin board. She looked a whole lot better today. She was rubbing her belly as she checked her phone, occasionally looking around.

I half wondered if I should say something to her. Maybe apologize for speaking to her out of the blue the other day. But just then, a tall man appeared from beyond the bulletin board. It was like some kind of TV drama on fast-forward. The man held out his hands reassuringly and made some comment. She laughed, notes like a xylophone spilling from her mouth. The two of them started walking up to the top of the hill.

Without waiting for them to disappear from view, I turned around and retraced my steps down the sloping road back to my apartment. Then a thought struck me: I hadn't talked to a single soul the whole weekend.

The end-of-year office party had no real beginning and no end. It simply dragged on under soporific orange lighting. Edamame, karaage, tamagoyaki, senbei. Sad-looking excuses for snacks, wilted leftovers that nobody could be bothered to finish, and over them, strands of conversation ran on, occasionally getting tangled up, before finally sinking into a haze of alcohol and cigarettes. The usual gripes about the factory and our clients, stories of parties of yesteryear, talk about the latest health craze and why this one's so different. And of course everyone's favorite subject: food.

I gave my belly a little scratch. Today I'd stuffed my dress with a scarf. The raging appetite I'd had going into my second trimester had dropped off a little, and my walks seemed to have brought my weight more or less back to what it had been before. Still, I thought it was important that my belly stick out just a bit, so I'd been stuffing something inside my clothes every day. I'd been checking Baby-N-Me to see what size the fetus should be each week and adjusting accordingly. This week, it's supposed to be the size of a mango. I went with an old woolen scarf, but this turned out to be a bad idea. The air in the izakaya was uncomfortably warm. My stomach was drenched with sweat. Itchy, too.

"Hey, Shibata . . . so you're, uh . . ."

"I'm what?" I asked, turning to look straight at the person who was talking to me. It was Tanaka. The lenses of his thick-rimmed glasses looked vaguely white. I could see a greasy finger mark on them, even from across the table.

The tables around us were occupied by my coworkers, all talking loudly. Since so many companies were having parties, we couldn't get a private room. Instead we were seated six to a table, all in one section of the izakaya. At the other end of a table diagonally opposite me, my section head was holding court. Every time he told some joke, everybody around him would screech with laughter and clap their hands like cymbal-banging monkeys.

"You're pregnant . . . aren't you?"

"Uh-huh."

"Well, are you going to tell us? Is it a boy or a girl?"

"I don't know yet. . . ."

"It's gonna be a girl. Pretty sure of it . . ."

A girl. And who was this guy to tell me what my imaginary baby was going to be? Higashinakano's convinced it'll be a boy, I was about to say, but decided not to bother. Higashinakano wasn't here today: he'd come down with the flu. It didn't seem like a severe strain this year, but he'd been one of the first in the office to catch it. In the elevator in the morning I'd heard somebody expressing irritation that he'd chosen the busiest time of the year to get sick.

You're just not the type who would have a boy, Shibata. Yeah, it's gonna be a girl. Tanaka repeated this several times, then called over a waitress, who probably wasn't Japanese, and after taking an insanely long time, ordered a beer. The other two at our table seemed to have gone off to the bathroom.

Large platters of fried rice were brought to each of the tables, along with small bowls with half a dozen porcelain rice spoons rattling around inside them. Tanaka stopped and just stared at the big platter in front of him until I took his bowl and filled it with rice. He took it from me, almost grunting his thanks, then immediately dug in, grains of rice spilling from his bowl.

"Seriously, though. You of all people, Shibata . . ."

"Me of all people?"

"Yeah, I mean . . . it's just a shock. . . . The shock of the year, for sure."

The others who'd been sitting with us returned to their seats. Some other guy I didn't know went into the bathroom. The door swung open, and I caught sight of a Peace Boat poster hanging on the other side of the door.

"Hey, is it cool if I touch your bump? Hahaha," Tanaka said with a smile. I remained silent. "Sorry, I'm just playing around." I didn't say anything back, and he returned to shoveling rice into his mouth. Yellow grains were getting everywhere: the table, the front of his shirt, around the ring on his left hand. There was a grease stain on his dark blue shirt.

"It's just so weird, you know? To think of you with a kid."

"You mean, I don't look like someone who would want children?"

"No, that's not what I'm saying. . . ." Tanaka brought his beer mug to his lips with one hand as he scratched his stomach with the other. Bits of rice dropped to the floor.

"You guys are surprised, too, right? About Shibata being pregnant?" he asked the two men who'd rejoined us.

The two men looked at each other with smiles that gave nothing away. One of them was the youngest guy in the section, and the other one was maybe a couple of years older than I was. The older one said, "Well, yeah, I definitely didn't see it coming. . . ." Then the younger one nodded. "Yeah, I guess I was pretty surprised," he said, then added, "but congratulations. Good for you." Then he downed his whiskey highball in one go. Drips of condensation from the bottom of his mug joined the stray bits of rice on the table. The older one took my oshibori and used it to gather the grains in a little pile and wipe them up. I didn't say anything. I just drank my oolong tea.

Tanaka kept his eyes fixed on the others, taking the occasional swig of beer while they devoured their rice, then suddenly leaned over, bringing his face uncomfortably close to mine. His glasses looked even dirtier up close.

"It's just hard to wrap my head around it. It's so weird to think of you being pregnant. I mean, I've never heard you say anything about love or marriage. That's why it was such a surprise to find out that you've been . . . getting out there, you know? Having a life."

I watched as my oshibori, left on the table's edge, fell to the floor and got stepped on as someone walked by.

"Hard to wrap your head around it?" I said. "Of course I have a life! You don't know the first thing about me, and I don't know anything about you, not that I want to. You wanna see me give birth? Is that what you're saying? That's the only way you'll ever be able to wrap your head around me having a kid of my own, right?"

But maybe I have one of those voices that doesn't carry. Tanaka didn't appear to have heard a thing, and simply called the waitress over again. He made some stupid comment about the foreign name on her badge, laughed, then ordered three highballs and—without even asking—ordered me a green tea. The waitress brought the drinks, with the same smile on her face. One table over, I overheard the group rambling on about school reunions.

"Um . . ." I began.

That moment, the emcee clapped his hands. "Hey,

everybody! Listen up! The section head's going to give the final speech of the night!"

The three men looked at me before turning their attention to the section head. Tanaka set his mug down on the table. I stared for a while at the layer of foam on his beer, bubbles rising to the surface only to vanish. I looked up again.

"The company's gonna give me the usual money when the baby's born . . . even if I'm not married . . . right?" I let out one loud breath after another, hoping it might sound like a laugh, but nobody seemed to know what to say. "I'm sure they will," Tanaka eventually said under his breath. "You should talk to General Affairs."

Then the section head launched into his speech. "We still have a few days to go before the year ends, but thanks for your hard work. I'm so glad all of us could make it here to welcome the coming year together, despite the rising cost of materials, so many clients going out of business, tumultuous transformations in the industry. . . ."

Someone got up and went to the bathroom, and I caught another glimpse of that same poster. Right then, I really did want to be on that ship, on some ocean somewhere, far away from all this.

Slipping away from a group of coworkers who were heading off to their own after-party, and walking on for a bit, I found myself on a shopping street in Ginza. It was a little after ten. I stepped inside a dazzlingly bright convenience store, bought myself a can of beer, and, after tossing the receipt in the trash by the entrance, set off again, sipping as I walked. The beer went down my throat and right to my head. I felt a tiny charge of electricity rise up through my heels with every step, and new colors flickered behind my eyelids. Finally, some alcohol.

Ginza on a December night. There was no escaping the bright lights. People flowed from one place to the next, like shoals of fish. Floating in their alcohol-laden breath were memories rising to the surface, snatches of gossip, grievances never to be resolved, desires openly expressed, momentary temptations. The intersection was packed, no different from daytime. People's consciousness and the heat of their bodies mingled, images emerged out of nowhere as if from a magic lantern, soothing you if you turned one way, striking you across the face if you turned another. Feeling drunk, as if I had to be hallucinating, I walked on, drawn forward by the massive displays of lights, past windows full of twinkling presents and golden teddy bears. And then I found myself standing in front of a building on a street that was almost totally deserted.

The building was narrow. Just a wedge squeezed in between another building covered top to bottom with logos, and an old pawn shop that had definitely seen better days. The first and second floors seemed to be a shop for kids' books, with banners advertising collections of children's literature, but the light in all of the windows was long gone now, and the door, which was covered in a pattern of vine leaves, was shut tight. The windows on the fourth floor, the building's highest, were colored: they looked like stained glass. The light of the moon seemed to be homing in on parts of the windows that were trying to hide themselves in the darkness, lighting up a woman's figure at the center of a tableau. My eyes met hers. She was holding a baby, and behind her I could see three distinguished-looking figures. Of course—it was her, that famous mother.

You didn't have it easy, did you? I heard myself saying.

It must have been so hard. Finding out you were pregnant, no idea how it happened, then getting visited by those angels or whatever. Your morning sickness was probably pretty bad, too. I can only imagine what that was like. And you were really young, weren't you? Everyone around you must have been so shocked. I bet some people just thought you'd slept with some-body and didn't want to say anything. And your husband-to-be, Joseph . . . He was a shepherd, right? Or was he a carpenter? I can't remember. What did he do when he found out? Was he pissed off? Sorry, I guess I don't actually know the story that well. . . .

But listen, I'm doing this thing right now where I'm pretending to be pregnant. I don't think you'd ap-prove. You'd tell me to stop, wouldn't you? No angels or wise men are going to come and visit me. I haven't even told my parents. . . . But the reaction I get at work is pure disbelief. They tell me they can't "wrap their heads around it." But what makes them think they can say that? I don't know them and they don't know me. . . . I mean—

The sudden squeal of brakes, followed by the sound of an engine revving.

A taxi came out of a narrow alley, heading straight for me. There was no sign of it slowing down. I stumbled, but managed to get out of the way. The car caught the edge of my coat as it sped past. I was fine, but it left me in a state of shock. The car kept going, racing up the road as if nothing had happened.

I went back to staring at the road in silence. Still not a soul to be seen. Then I heard voices. Laughter. It wasn't one person, or even two: it was a whole group. Gradually, the voices grew louder, and finally the revelers appeared. There were maybe ten of them. They seemed to be drunk, making their way up the road in my direction, lurching and swaying, their silhouettes reminding me of wobble toys. They all had elf hats on. Green and red stripes flashed in the darkness, like some sort of code. The woman walking at the front of the group, with legs like a flamingo's, pointed up at the street sign and screamed out something in a shrill voice. Everyone burst into even louder laughter. I could almost smell the alcohol on their breath. Somebody whistled, a piercing note that broke through the silence of the night.

I knew I had to get away from them. I didn't want to have anything to do with them—or with anyone, really. But I resented having to leave. I wanted to keep communing with *her*.

I turned my back to them and grabbed my phone

from my bag. Taking my time, trying to appear casual, like I was waiting for a friend, I braced myself, kept my gaze down at my feet. I pressed some buttons on my phone. As the too-bright screen came up, shining straight into my eyes, I knew they'd just about reached me. I felt a tap on my shoulder. I gave a strangled hiccup.

"Merry Christmas!" It was the woman with the flamingo legs. She screeched these words, looking right at me. In her startlingly clear eyes, I caught a glimpse of my own reflection. There I was, looking like an idiot, staring on for all eternity.

Merry Christmas! Merry Christmas!

The rest of the group called out, one after another as they passed me. It seemed like a strange medley of people—men and women, young and old. Their blessings rang out in the quiet winter's night. As they disappeared up the road, the last of them turned back, then mimed to me, rubbing his belly and clapping his hands without making a sound. A tiny little encore.

And with that, the procession of midnight saints wended its way out of my sight.

Sometime after the street had returned to silence, I tried saying it myself.

Merry Christmas.

I looked up again at the stained glass window. There she was, the same smile on her lips.

I'm sure you were totally freaked out when they told you that you were pregnant, but at least your baby's birth is now celebrated all around the world! And so many people have been saved by you, and by your child! Then again, to be eternally known as the Virgin Mother, as if that's the only thing that gave meaning to your existence . . . Hey, did you have any hobbies of your own? Or maybe there was a singer you were really into? You must have gotten stressed out sometimes. I mean, being called the Virgin Mother, even after your son was all grown up . . . And then to have him crucified like that. I can't imagine how hard that must have been. I just hope you managed to live your life the way you wanted, to take naps when you felt like it, to know yourself by a name that made sense to you. . . .

I suddenly noticed my own white reflection in the building's windows. I turned to face myself and stuck out my belly. Congratulations! I whispered to myself. Just to see what it felt like.

After a little wave of my hand to the woman in the stained glass above me, I headed to the station. I let my shoulders drop, and the night air filled my lungs.

The old buildings, the asphalt, the air around me—everything twinkled as if packed with constellations of light.

Here was the entrance to the subway, tucked away behind a line of weeping willows. After listening to the distant noise from the main road for a moment or two, I walked down the steps, into the belly of the station.

Once I was home, I opened up a nonalcoholic beer and made myself a simple bowl of nyumen along with some kiriboshi daikon that I'd cooked earlier and some strips of steamed chicken. I needed real food, not sad-looking izakaya snacks, if I was going to say anything that people could hear. I opened up Baby-N-Me and recorded the details of my meals and exercise for the day. Under exercise, I wrote, "Walking, two stations' worth."

The first chapter in my own blue-light bible.

WEEK 20

○————————————————○

"Hey, when are you going to clean out your old room?
All those comics, and the clothes you never took with
you? Your brother's coming tomorrow, with Satomi
and the kids. . . ."

"Yeah, I know," I said. And then: "But it's not like
they're going to be here in the morning, right?"

I grabbed the ladle, took some meat and vegetables
from the hotpot and put them into my dish, then
skimmed off the scum while I was at it. It had spread
out over the surface like a field of pampas grass. Neither my dad nor my mom seemed to have noticed.

My dad apparently didn't recognize any of the
singers appearing on *Kohaku* this year, so he switched
channels a few times, but failing to find anything of
interest, he returned to the singing contest and filled
his glass with beer. It looked like he didn't want any
more meat. My mom hadn't had much of anything at

all. The old clock on the wall chimed, filling the tiny kitchen with its ridiculously loud sound, and at the same moment a group of idols I'd never seen before burst into song. Hurrying to bring the volume down, my dad pressed the wrong button on the remote and a commentator's voice came on over the music. In the next moment, an electronic melody blared from across the house telling us the laundry was dry. The little scene of three adults sitting around the dinner table had turned into a kind of hell.

When I'd first arrived at the house, I put down my overnight bag in the hallway, stopped for a moment to loosen the scarf that I'd wound up over my face, and almost fainted. Countless white faces were floating before me in the darkness of the stairs.

My mom, in her white apron, popped her face out of the kitchen doorway.

"Careful on your way up. I put the dolls out so they could get some air."

They were my old dolls from Girls' Day and my brother's from Boys' Day. They were on every step of the old wooden staircase, staring down into the freezing cold of the hallway. I made my way upstairs, lifting my arms so that the hem of my coat wouldn't knock over any dolls: the emperor, the empress, a few baby-faced warriors, then the three court ladies. I felt my sock brush up against something and looked down to find a few old guys I couldn't name on their sides. I quickly helped them up.

The line of figures went all the way to the top of the stairs. On the bookshelf, the five court musicians had been divided up—placed in whatever space was left between *The Family Medical Encyclopedia* and my old set of Harry Potter books. Well, I guess no band lasts forever.

As soon as I set down my things, I heard my mom call for me to come back down. I headed downstairs, passing the dolls yet again. Hey, I feel bad. I know you guys were praying for me year after year. But maybe it just wasn't meant to be, you know? It's the child's wishes that are important, after all, not the parents'. Next time you choose a family, maybe you should give some more thought to the kid's wishes? I looked back up at them from the bottom of the stairs. The dolls didn't agree or fight back.

The hallway downstairs was bone-chillingly cold. I wondered if my dad was watching TV, so I looked in and saw the TV set talking cheerfully to a table with nothing but an unfinished sudoku on it—nobody around. I clicked off the TV and went into the living room, which obviously hadn't been used for a pretty long time, then headed straight back out into the hall-way. Even though I was indoors, my breath was showing white, but as soon as I opened the kitchen door, I was hit in the face by the smell of soy sauce and the heat of something being grilled. My mom, standing in front of the stove, turned and looked at me.

"Sorry. I've got my hands full with this. Dad's taking his bath now. You can get in after him."

My mom's busy hands looked bony as they gripped the cooking chopsticks. Meanwhile, the carrots and snow peas simmering in the skillet seemed so full of the promise of life.

I helped myself to some cookies, borrowed my mom's padded jacket, and perused the newspaper until it was my turn to get in the bath. A newspaper printed on actual paper. When was the last time I saw one of these? And it was a local newspaper, too. The print seemed larger. Two elderly people in town had choked to death on mochi they'd managed to sneak past the nursing home staff. . . . It wasn't even New Year's yet, but they'd already gotten into the mochi? Was that all there was to look forward to in the end?

I could imagine how old people might feel like the week or so from Christmas to New Year's was totally unbearable. The days on the calendar just rolling by, nothing to do, nothing to look forward to. Like some kind of weird dream with no exit.

"Hey, mind if I break into this matsumaezuke?" my dad asked as he opened the fridge, looking for something to snack on.

"Wait until tomorrow, when everyone's here. Besides, didn't you say you had ozenzai after lunch? Remember what the doctor said last time."

Casting one final glance at my dad's back as he peered into the fridge, I headed into the bath. So big, so white, and so incredibly hot . . . I looked at the unfamiliar bottles of shampoo and liquid body soap, brands I never saw in the stores in Tokyo. As I stretched out in the tub, a spot of mold next to the bath control panel caught my eye.

How long have you been in your apartment now?"

"Um . . . Six years?"

My mom split open a block of tofu with her chopsticks. As soon as my dad left the dining table to unwind in the other room with beer and snacks, my mom started taking things out of the pot to eat. After dousing her food in an unbelievable amount of ponzu, she opened up a can of chuhai. Want some? I'm okay, thanks. I haven't had anything to drink since last week.

"How's work?"

"Same as usual."

My mom leaned forward to grab the serving chopsticks. The skin of her scalp gleamed white under the lamp. Her hair had grown so thin. I decided I'd send her some good shampoo for her next birthday. I handed her the chopsticks, then reached under the table and switched the burner to high.

"Your company's better than most. They give you a housing allowance, right? I bet there aren't many people who leave once they start working there."

"I guess you're right."

"But your brother . . . He's barely keeping his head above water. It was hard enough with just Hiroto, but when they had Haruna last year . . . Of course, they're lucky to have children and all that, but . . . Did you see the dolls upstairs? Remember them? I thought the kids could take them tomorrow."

I wondered if my brother and his wife knew that this gift was coming their way. I remembered the blue compact car that my brother and his family drove over from the next prefecture every year. My nephew, sitting in the back, surrounded by piles of stuffed animals, waving until the very last.

"People these days . . . Raising kids when they don't have enough to look after them. . . . It's got to be tough. Well, I guess if you're having kids, you gotta do it early. . . ."

Yeah, pregnancy is hard. I nodded.

My mom had apparently lost interest in the hot-pot. She started telling me about the hula lessons she'd been taking at the civic center. "Look," she said. She put her plate down, got up, and gave me a little demonstration. She was actually pretty good. She'd gotten hooked on some burdock root tea that somebody she'd met in the class told her about. Next time, she said, she'd order some for me and send it to Tokyo.

When "Auld Lang Syne" started playing in the next room, my mom went to the freezer and got some ice cream. Cups of Häagen-Dazs.

How long had it been since I'd had ice cream? I'd hardly had any since I started living on my own.

"Nothing hits the spot like a little ice cream, right?" My mom had her own cup, but she kept digging her spoon into mine, telling me that I wouldn't be able to finish it on my own. Every time she licked the Peter Rabbit spoon, it left pink streaks on the back. When she smiled, the silver crowns on her back teeth caught the light. After finishing her ice cream, she got up and grabbed a magazine, I thought maybe to read it, but no. An old classmate of mine from elementary school was in it, and she wanted me to see. Remember her? Such a pretty girl . . . Sorry, Mom, it doesn't ring a bell. She babbled away for a little bit longer, then cleaned up, brushed her teeth, and disappeared off to bed without even waiting for midnight.

Left alone in the kitchen, I finished off the rest of my ice cream. It tasted all the sweeter in a warm room. I dipped my spoon over and over into the melted ice cream at the bottom of the cup as I drank tea from a Snoopy mug. Peter Rabbit, Snoopy, Doraemon, Hello Kitty . . . Everywhere I looked, I saw ghosts, still stuck here in this old house, even though my brother and I had grown up and left years ago.

Once I washed the cup and spoon I'd been using, I turned off the kitchen light and walked out into the hallway. The freezing, damp air coming up through the old floorboards made me hunch my shoulders. As I walked toward the stairs, I heard the sound of the

TV. My dad had evidently stuck with *Kohaku* until the very end.

My old bedroom was now my mom's sewing room. Whenever I made trips back to see my parents, I stayed in the room that they used to hang the laundry. As I laid out the bedding, which smelled of mothballs, I heard shouts and cheers from far away, followed once again by silence. Looking at my phone, I saw that the old year had given way to the new.

"Happy New Year!" I said out loud. I was well into my pregnancy now. It was about the time when I was supposed to start talking to the baby.

Thirty-four years on this earth, but I couldn't remember anything about how I'd spent the first few days of any January. It was a blank. Every year when it was time to go back to school or work, I'd reach for my bag and sling it over my shoulder, feeling the strap dig in, then run out of the house, straight uphill, worried that I was going to be late. . . . Short of breath, cold but hot. The sight of all the black and gray coats as they streamed down into the subway always made me want to turn back, but I'd get sucked down along with them. As a gray mist filled my field of vision, it would hit me. Here I was again, doing exactly what I did the year before.

But maybe this year would be different. A year to remember.

"Shibata. Did you find out?" Higashinakano asked me. It was the afternoon, and only a few people were at their desks. He was practically whispering, like a kid asking me if I had a crush on a classmate.

"Find out what?"

"You know . . . Is it a boy or a girl?"

I forgot. I did say I might find out at some point. My attention was suddenly drawn to his ear hair, growing wild like weeds. When I turned away and looked out the window, it was white with condensation.

"If you don't want to say, that's absolutely fine. . . ."

"It's a boy."

The creases around the corners of Higashinakano's eyes deepened.

"Hey! What did I tell you?" he said as his whole face broke into a smile. "I just had this feeling, you know? That's wonderful news! Of course, it would be great if you were having a girl, too. . . ."

Several people turned to look at us. Higashinakano had a real problem with volume control. My back felt hot. I got up, opened the window, and looked outside. The air was as clear as could be. Everywhere I looked, I saw the icy cool colors of winter. *It's a boy, it's a boy.* Maybe if I said it to myself enough times, if I really prayed for it, it just might . . .

Around the end of the holidays, I realized that my belly was a little bigger. That made sense, considering all the kabukiage I'd eaten back home. Those things can really mess up the inside of your mouth. My mom was always saying so. But there was something else to it. There was this force I could feel inside me.... Over the holidays, I'd taken a break from stuffing my clothes. But now, when I went to put my scarf under my dress, I felt a presence that I hadn't felt before.

I needed to do something to keep my weight down. Evening walks didn't seem to be cutting it. On the final day of the holiday break, I stopped by a gym. The woman behind the counter, long and thin like kanpyo strips, handed me a flyer before I could even open my mouth. "Congratulations!" she said. The flyer was for a prenatal yoga class. When I got home and looked into it a little, I found out that I could get a discount through work.

The next day, my first day back in the office, I got back to my desk after a quick bathroom break to find a huge bundle of New Year's cards waiting there for me. I sighed softly. Right. I forgot. It was up to me to sort these and deliver them throughout the office, then write replies to any cards addressed to my section.

But before I knew it, some other tasks came my way, and I ended up just shoving the cards into my pocket. Toward the end of the day, when I remembered them, they were no longer there. Looking around, wondering where I might have lost them, I heard Tanaka complaining about something, and a couple of minutes later I saw him walking around the office, leaving cards on people's desks. Lucky me!

Friday afternoon. After a visit to a client, I decided not to go back to the office, and headed straight home. It was early, well before five o'clock. The rain that had been falling all day was beginning to let up. Waiting for the train, I folded up my collapsible umbrella and noticed a patch of sky behind the clouds. It was the color of vodka sauce.

It had been only a few hours since I stepped out of the train onto this platform on my way to see the client. It was brand new, spotless, and pretty much deserted. Apart from the station announcements, the only thing I heard was an elderly lady talking to a man in a wheelchair. The man wasn't really listening; he just stared off, looking nowhere in particular, but the woman kept talking as if that didn't bother her. I kind of watched them, wondering if I'd ever come to this station again. As a train pulled in, this melody started playing over the speakers, the kind of song they have in an RPG when the hero is about to set out on their big adventure.

On the train, a girl who was probably in high school offered me her seat. I thanked her and sat down. Her hair was really short, and I could see a sailor suit under her bomber jacket. That brought me back. Her skirt, which swayed as she stood up, just brushed her knees. She'd been sitting with her backpack between her legs, but now she threw it over her shoulder. She reached out and ran her fingers through the hair of the girl sitting next to me.

"Hey, want some kanyu drops?"

"Kanyu drops?"

"You didn't have those back in kindergarten? Cod liver oil. They're kinda like candy, but sour."

"Yeah, I know what they are, but why do you have them?"

The girl asking—the one sitting next to me—craned her neck out of her light pink scarf. As she looked up, I found myself fascinated by the length of her eyelashes.

"Hold out your hand."

Something moved from one white hand to another. It was lavender and looked almost weightless. The girl sitting next to me opened her palm to reveal a piece of paper in the shape of an animal with four stubby legs—something between a bear and a dog.

"It's a badger."

The girl who was standing grabbed some origami squares from her backpack pocket. "Pretty cool, huh?"

"I want something else. Something cuter. And what about the kanyu drops?"

"My little brother brought this back from school yesterday. He said he didn't want them. Let's make something."

"That's okay. What about the drops?"

"Here, it's simple. . . ."

The girl who was standing put an orange square in the other girl's lap, and then took out a dark green sheet for herself and started explaining what to do. First, make a triangle. I followed along in my mind, folding my square into a triangle.

"Go slower or I can't follow. Also . . ."

". . . Also?"

"I ate grasshoppers yesterday," the girl sitting next to me said, then carefully folded the sheet in her lap into a perfect triangle. Two badgers started to take shape.

The train crossed a large river. A sudden break in the built-up areas, then immediately a panorama of houses and apartments stretching out before my eyes. Under the all-too-pale light of the sun, the train crawled across the land. Then I realized I had no idea where I was supposed to get off.

WEEK 23

As soon as I told Higashinakano it was a boy, he started asking me, at least once every three days, whether I'd decided on a name. My attempts to head him off—"I'm still thinking about it," "I'd better wait until I see his face"—only made him more insistent. But once the baby comes, he'd say, you won't have the time to give it any real thought. . . .

On Tuesday, he was out of the office. I was leaving a memo on his desk when I spotted a piece of paper with my name on it among his notebooks. Before I knew it, I'd taken it.

I went back to my desk and unfolded it. It was a single page torn from a notebook. It was soft like leather, probably because it had been folded over so many times. At the top was my name, SHIBATA, in big characters, followed by a long list of boys' names in small writing that filled the page. Each name had a number next to it, presumably the stroke count, and several names had red circles around them.

I put the list back on Higashinakano's desk. It was essential that I choose a name before Higashinakano chose one for me. Any name would do, as long as it sounded convincing enough. There was a bookstore not too far from the office. At lunch, I headed straight there to check out the maternity magazines.

It turns out that a wide variety of factors come into play when picking a name for a baby. How it sounds, the meaning of the kanji . . . These were obvious. But some people gave a lot of thought to the number of strokes, took a character from their own name, or made some reference to the season of the baby's birth. I had to wonder about some of the things I was reading. For example, the idea that names that start with *s* sound "soft," and names that start with *m* sound "manly." That didn't sound right to me. I'd come across tons of *s* names that didn't sound soft at all. One magazine was saying that seasonal references were really popular these days. Well, that probably did make it easier to explain where your name came from. My brother was born on Ocean Day and my parents named him Kaito, with the characters for "ocean" and "person," but he ended up hating it. He had never learned to swim, despised summer, and all the kids at school were always calling him "Aquaman."

I kept reading. "What kind of person do you want your baby to be? Make a list of personality traits, have your husband do the same, then share what you came up with." There was a cartoon of a woman with a big belly, sitting on a sofa. "I want my boy to be considerate of others!" read the speech bubble by her head. A man, presumably her husband, was sitting next to her. His speech bubble read, "I want him to be strong and ambitious!" A cat lay at his feet.

As someone without a husband or a cat, I stood there thinking as I held the magazine in my hands. What kind of person do I want my baby to be? If I'm really going to have a baby . . . I thought about it for a while but couldn't make up my mind. Who was I to determine what kind of person someone else should become? I gave my belly a stroke, but no answer came from the padding.

I could think of plenty of things that I didn't want him to be. Someone with no imagination, somebody who was arrogant, who was incompetent. Someone who didn't listen to anybody else. Then again, if he was too sensitive, he was never going to be happy. . . . I didn't want a child with messy handwriting, even if nobody writes anything by hand these days. . . . It would be great if he had nicer eyes than I did. Big bright eyes.

I put the magazine back on the rack, took out my notebook, and began to sketch a face. Okay, maybe I can live with eyes that aren't really big and bright. Why overdo it? On the whole, best to avoid features that are too striking. Lips not too full, nose not too high. Eyebrows not too bushy, and well-defined. Maybe even a little beauty spot under one eye . . . Hmm. Not bad.

For his voice . . . Nothing too deep, I think. Not with this face. Also, he shouldn't talk too fast. If anything, he should be calm and relaxed. But intelligent. He shouldn't discriminate against others because of gender, age, or ethnicity. I don't want him to shout. He should be humble, really listen to people. He's got to have enough self-respect not to fawn. He should be moderately sociable, but also reasonably skeptical. I wrote out a list of qualities next to the face.

As I wrote in my notebook, I wondered: How many other imaginary children were there in the world? And where were they now? What were they doing? I hoped they were leading happy lives.

When I got out of the elevator, jam-packed with people coming back from lunch, I approached my desk and saw Higashinakano wrap up his bento box before putting it away. That piece of paper was laid out on his desk. Was he thinking about it again?

"Hey, just so you know, I've decided on a name," I said before he could get anything out. I pretended not to see the paper. "His name's going to be Sorato. Sorato Shibata. Sorato, with two kanji: the first for 'sky,' or 'air,' like 'out of thin air,' and the second for 'person.'"

Higashinakano repeated the name over and over under his breath, then wrote it out in the space between us with his finger and nodded, a pleased look on his face.

"Sorato. Sorato Shibata. Yes! What a wonderful name!"

WEEK 24

As the end of January approached, I was getting even bigger, and I started losing my balance. My center of gravity had shifted, and even when I was simply walking along a level surface, I'd find myself stumbling and would have to stop and steady myself. I'd stand there and hold my belly, with a vision of myself flat on the floor. And this wasn't just on the odd occasion. It happened when I was walking down the shallow steps at the subway station, or when I stepped out onto my balcony.

Baby-N-Me confirmed that the bigger your belly, the greater the risk of falling. Hard falls were to be avoided, so excessive weight gain was a no-no. That was it: I had to join that gym. I'd always wanted to try yoga anyway, and I had that discount through work. It was going to be cheap.

But when I showed the discount card from work

to the kanpyo lady at the counter, a regretful look crossed her face. The maternity yoga class was apparently extremely popular, and only available at full price. I'd have to pay for it. "But," she said, grabbing a brochure and holding it out for me, "you could always come to this."

"Aerobics?" I blurted out. In elementary school, I often came home to find my mom dancing in front of the TV. Hoping to lose weight without my dad knowing, she'd bought some fitness videos. I'd watch from the kitchen, snacking on a steamed bun or a cookie that she'd baked for me, while she tried to move to the music, always just behind the beat.

Did she get bored and give up? Or was it just that I started getting home later?

"This is maternity aerobics. The moms say it really helps keep off those extra pounds. It's open to anyone in their second or third trimester."

"It's my first time. Do you think I can keep up?"

"It's maternity aerobics. It's new for everyone. You'll be fine."

When I finished filling out the forms, the kanpyo lady slipped a bunch of documents into a folder and handed it to me. The words I saw jumped out.

MOMMY AEROBICS. Goodbye, Pregnancy Blues! Hello, Comfortable Birth! A Healthy Happy Pregnancy Means a Healthy Happy Baby. . . .

At first I thought I'd wandered into some kind of rural festival celebrating the arrival of spring. As soon as I opened the door to the studio, I saw a throng of pregnant women dressed up in bright T-shirts: green, orange, red. A few were even wearing bra tops.

"Yeah, but I got *two* on the way!" A voice came flying over from behind me.

Ever since I got pregnant, I'd been watching other pregnant women at the station or the supermarket, and sometimes I'd catch sight of a group of two or maybe three moms-to-be, but I'd never seen so many of them gathered together in one place before. The women in this room were bursting with laughter, chatting away as if completely liberated. . . . How a polar bear that had spent its whole life inside some tiny cage at the zoo would probably act if released into the wild.

The only people who weren't talking away were me and one other woman who was just sitting quietly on her mat. She was obviously overweight, and she had her hair in thick braids that hung down over her shoulders. Her thick glasses made her look naive, almost childlike, but the huge belly pushing out from under her bright neon-blue T-shirt was plain to see.

She's got a baby in there. I gulped nervously as I looked around. All these other women with bumps of all sizes. Beneath their colorful shirts and soft skin were little, defenseless babies. I stroked my own belly. A bit of cold air ran up the arm of my T-shirt. I wasn't using any of the usual padding.

A few minutes before class, a woman dressed in white entered the room and started checking our blood pressure and weight. Everybody kept talking while they waited. When it was my turn, I pulled out the registration card that I'd just gotten at the counter. The woman took the card and flashed a smile. "First time, huh?" There were white streaks in her boyishly short hair. As I filled in my weight and a few other details, I got a tap on the shoulder.

"You're looking pretty slim for twenty-four weeks in. But that's okay. I see tons of pregnant women every day, so I know. Your delivery's gonna be easy. You've got the hips for it. As long as you eat well, sleep well, and come to aerobics, your baby's gonna be as healthy as can be!"

But what a workout. There was no way anyone, let alone a pregnant woman, could keep this up.

The warm-up stretches were fine. We started out nice and gentle, with people making occasional comments about how it felt so good, or maybe hurt just a little. Hey, I can definitely handle this, I thought. Then the stretches ended and the instructor told us to take a water break. From then on, people became less talkative. Next came step practice, with everybody moving while the instructor clapped her hands, and I could feel something changing in the room, like all the air was getting sucked out. Then, when the music was suddenly cranked up, I finally understood. The beat controls everything here. When the overhead lights were dimmed and the mirror ball started to twirl, the studio revealed its true nature and became a nightclub.

The bass took over, making the whole studio vibrate and my belly shake. We started with light steps, but as the music surged and everyone started clapping, we moved on to doing squats, which we followed up with even more intense stepping, then ultimately broke into some truly hard-core dance moves. Nobody was talking now. And how could we? All we could do was keep moving our legs, arms, and heads. Nice and high! Reach for the ceiling, ladies! Up, up, up! The instructor, who had started out in a T-shirt and leggings, was now practically naked. "If it's even a little too much, go ahead and take a break," she yelled, but every time someone started to slow down, she'd walk over, put her hand on their shoulder, and ask with a big smile, "You doing okay?" Her thin arms had the thickest veins I'd ever seen.

In the mirrors that covered the studio from floor to ceiling, big-bellied women kept dancing with dead-serious looks on their faces. As the steps grew more and more intense, the floor started to shake. Of course it did. There were actually twice as many people in the room as you could see. In the light coming off the mirror ball, the beads of sweat on our faces shone like diamonds. Halfway through class, my knees started to give, but in this studio, stopping was never an option—not while the beat was going. The instructor's voice rang out: "Let's go, ladies! One! Two! Three! One! More! Time!"

Utterly dominated by the thudding music, everybody was dancing madly, but the one who was dancing the maddest was the woman in the neon-blue shirt. While everybody else looked sapped, barely managing to keep up with the instructor, she let out a roar like an animal, her breasts shaking like a pair of fruits as she sensually thrust out her belly over and over. It was like she was dancing at some harvest festival. The more she moved, the faster the beat seemed to get.

The heat of the room entered my lungs, and just when I thought my arms and legs were about to fall off, the fierce beat came to a stop and gave way to the mellow sound of harp arpeggios. Our steps got slower and slower; the mirror ball stopped spinning. The next thing I knew, all these women with round bellies were on their backs and bathing in soft green light as if we were suddenly in some kind of forest. Deep breaths, everybody. In and out, in and out.

Have a great evening! Get home safe! The kanpyo lady called out as we exited the gym. Up ahead, walking toward the subway, I noticed the woman in the neon-blue shirt. With every step she took, her thick braids swung from side to side.

It was already getting dark. The Sunday evening air was crisp and cool. But when I closed my eyes, my eyelids felt hot. There was something warm moving inside me.

As I waited for the light to change, I pulled out my phone and opened Baby-N-Me. I plugged in today's exercise: MOMMY AEROBICS, 50 MIN.

WEEK 26

They had weekday evening classes, too. If I left the office on time, I could make it. And I could take as many classes as I wanted, so I thought I might as well go on the way home from work when I could. Last week, that was Tuesday and Thursday. I went a couple of times this week, too. It hadn't even been three weeks since I'd signed up, but my body was already changing, little by little. Whenever I got out of the bath and looked at my backside in the mirror, I could see a real difference in my hips and thighs. My core felt stronger, and I didn't feel like I was about to fall over all the time. My belly was getting bigger, and sometimes I felt a pain in my back, but it wasn't un-bearable. Honestly, I was feeling better than I ever had in my life.

I started watching movies on the days I didn't go to aerobics. I wanted to take advantage of my eve-nings at home while they lasted, so a couple of weeks ago I signed up for Amazon Prime. It was either that or Netflix, but in the end I decided I was in the mood to catch up on a bunch of older movies. Last week I watched *Midnight in Paris* and *One Flew over the Cuckoo's Nest*. Over the weekend I watched *Pulp Fiction*, *Blue*, and *Cinema Paradiso*. Sometimes I'll spend three or four days on a single movie, watching a little at a time, but some nights I'll go for a double feature.

I had aerobics today. It was about time for me to leave the office, and when I pulled out the bag I had my change of clothes in, I could feel Higashinakano staring. He kept walking behind me, back and forth, carrying a huge stack of paper. His little noises and the constant rustling of paper were too much, so eventually I turned around to look at him.

"What's in the bag?" Higashinakano asked, all smiles as he pointed at my tote. "You've been bringing that to work a lot lately."

Left with no other choice, I told him about the aerobics class for pregnant women. "Aerobics?!" He was so loud that I had to look around to see if Tanaka or the section head had heard. Fortunately, it was evening, and they were too busy to notice.

"That must be a pretty good workout."

DIARY OF A VOID

"Oh, there's nothing pretty about it."

"But it has to be a lot of fun."

"You think?"

"Sure! You're getting ready for Sorato, right?"

Sorato. I couldn't get my head around that name coming out of somebody else's mouth. I felt like I'd fallen asleep curled up on my armchair in the privacy of my living room, only to wake up and find myself dumped out on a crowded city street, no clue how I'd gotten there. I felt so exposed. But if I'd already come this far, what was stopping me from going anywhere I wanted? I could head straight to the airport and get on a plane to some foreign country, still in my pajamas.

Before I started this job, when I had some vacation time left over from my old one, I took a trip to Turkey. I could have gone anywhere in the world, but I went with Turkey. Remembering some white and dry landscape I'd seen once, maybe in a movie, I booked a flight and never looked back.

On Turkish streets, there was always music. Even when there was no actual song playing, I could hear music in the footsteps of children as they ran through the streets, and the voices filling the marketplace. They had a beat all their own. The air was rich with the smells of spices and cooking meat. I didn't give any thought to safety or language before I left, but once I'd found the rhythm of the place, I was fine. I slipped into my old sneakers and headed out to take in the magnificence of the mosques. I strode through the Grand Bazaar at night, and when I got tired of walking, I'd drink hot, strong Turkish tea. I couldn't really understand what anybody was saying, but I still felt like I got the gist of it. Plus, taking my shoes off indoors made me feel right at home.

The day before my flight back, I had breakfast and spent the morning walking around the places I'd liked best. In the afternoon, I figured I'd buy some gifts. I made my way around the little shops crowding the dusty alleys, doing so much walking that the soles of my shoes were worn down to practically nothing, and buying all the sweets I could get my hands on to give to friends back home. I was just about ready to walk back to the hotel for a quick nap before dinner when I stumbled upon a kilim shop down one of the alleys.

With every step I took, I felt the air getting cooler, the smell of perfume getting stronger. Peering inside

from the doorway, I saw countless rugs crammed together in the dark, each of them buzzing with some
kind of mystical geometry. Deep inside, I could see a
woman with dark skin dressed in black. She was writing something, but she stopped to look up when she
noticed me. She didn't say a word, but I could tell
from the look in her eyes that it was all right for me to
come inside.

As I entered, the scent became that much stronger.
Maybe the woman was burning incense. She returned
to her writing, and I started at one end, looking at
each kilim, unsure whether it was okay to touch them.
If they were outside, they'd be bursting with color,
but here in the dark, the patterns appeared to be
resting—maybe even plotting something.

Then one rug caught my eye. It wasn't really the
color or the design that grabbed me. In fact, at first
glance it looked pretty ordinary. It was the color of
dry brick—hardly what people imagine when they
hear the word "kilim"—but when I got closer, I could
see an intricate pattern of vines decorated with dancing reds gathered from flowers all around the world,
creating a garden known to no one. Without even re-
alizing it, I was tracing the lines with my finger. I
want to take this home, I thought. I want to own it.

But when I looked at the price tag hanging off the side, I knew that this kilim would never be mine. Converting liras to yen in my head, I found that it cost far more than my hotel room. I'd never spend that kind of money on something I was just going to lay under my feet.

I figured I should get going, but I didn't know whether I should say goodbye to the woman in black. As I tried to decide, my phone started ringing inside my shoulder bag. I hurried out into the alley, where I was enveloped by the smells and the sounds of the city.

"Hello?"

It was Yukino.

"Hey, sorry to call you up out of the blue. Are you done with work for the day? You home?"

"I'm in Turkey, looking at rugs."

"Huh?"

I explained how I'd decided to quit the company and was using up my vacation time. All the while worrying about how much this call was going to cost.

"So you're gonna buy a rug?" Yukino asked.

"I don't think so. The one I like's too expensive. How could I spend that much on something just to make my apartment look nice? It's not like I live with anybody anyway. . . ."

"Hmm . . . I dunno," Yukino said, then went quiet for a bit. I started wondering why she'd called. I wasn't sure whether I should ask or just get off the phone.

A couple—probably Europeans—walked by. They were eating what looked like crepes but probably weren't. The guy's wallet was popping out from the back pocket of his jeans for all the world to see, not that he seemed to mind.

"I don't know what 'expensive' is for you, or why it matters if you live on your own or not, but I think you should make your place look the way you want, before you forget what that is."

Yukino quickly added that she had no idea what my phone bill was going to be, but that I should tell her if it ended up being really bad, and then she hung up.

The European woman grabbed the guy's wallet and started waving it in the air, laughing her head off, while the guy pretended to be mad.

I'd been outside for only a couple of minutes, but as soon as I stepped back inside the shop, the dimness and smell of incense surrounded me, welcoming me back. When I picked up the brick-colored kilim and carried it over to the woman, who was still absorbed in her writing, she lifted her eyes and looked at me. I was convinced she'd been writing, but now I could see she'd actually been drawing in a corner of the ledger: an elaborate reproduction of the cash register on the counter and the ceramic sheep standing beside it, done using nothing but a ballpoint pen.

The woman hit a few keys on the register, and a number appeared on the display, much lower than what was written on the tag, not that she said anything about it. When I pulled out my credit card, she made no effort to conceal her annoyance, but she immediately grabbed a card reader from under the register. I caught sight of a pair of golden bracelets on her arm that clinked as she moved.

She didn't say a single word the whole time. Neither did I. When I stepped outside and swung the kilim onto my back, I turned around to look inside. The woman had gone back to her drawing.

That rug is in my living room to this day. At night, I lie on it when I do my pregnancy stretches. Or when I watch movies. Yesterday, I got started on *The Godfather*.

○------------○

"Hey. Ever use this stuff? It smells really nice. It's John Masters. Wanna try?"

More than the scent, what surprised me was the warmth of the brown bottle when she handed it to me. I usually couldn't stand it: the leftover heat from a train strap that somebody's been holding, or my office chair after someone's been sitting in it. But today it didn't bother me. Maybe because the locker room was a little less crowded than usual.

"Wow. This does smell nice."

"Right? Oil up. You'll get stretch marks no matter what, but you should do what you can. Know what I mean?"

I handed back the bottle, and the woman started putting oil on her own belly. I couldn't believe how round her belly was—or how thin her arms were. She rubbed the rest of the oil in her palms onto the sides of her thin, white face.

What was it about her face? I was sure I'd seen her somewhere before, but it wasn't coming to me. I finished changing, then reached into the locker for my sneakers. She did the same.

Hey, we said in unison. In our hands: two identical pairs of white leather Converse All Stars.

The woman turned to me. "Wanna come to the lounge? A bunch of us are hanging out there."

"The lounge?" I asked. Of course I knew about the lounge. Whenever I walked into the gym, I could see it through the glass, filled with people of all ages, but it hadn't ever occurred to me to step inside.

"Hey mamas!"

"Hosono! Are you getting skinnier? You know that's not how this works, right?"

"Yeah right! I'm twenty pounds heavier than I was before I got pregnant. I've never weighed so much in my whole life."

"That's nothing! I'm thirty over what I was."

"Hey Curly, pass me that phone?"

In between a group of older ladies debating the merits of dyeing their hair and a pair of older men with their heads buried in magazines, saying nothing,

five women about my age were sitting around a couple
of white plastic tables that they'd pulled together—
the kind they have in food courts—with a few drinks
and some snacks spread out in the middle.

As Hosono (that was her name, apparently) and I
walked over, they made room for us.

"Hey, whose are those?" Hosono asked, pointing
at the sweets. "They look really good."

"Mine! I've got this bakery by my house with the
most amazing bread. I've been going there a lot lately.
They've always got these incredible little desserts. Today they had these an-doughnuts," one woman said
before taking a bite. "Have some, have some," she said,
looking at me. She was chubby with a little face and
fine features. Her makeup was so perfect—every blem-
ish filled in—that you'd never guess she'd been covered
in sweat just a few minutes ago. I wondered how long it
had been since I'd talked to somebody with fake eyelashes.

"Sorry . . . what's your name?"

"Shibata."

"Shibata!" the group repeated after me. Then came
a torrent of questions: When are you due? Where do
you live? Was this your first class here? It was as if I'd
entered a birdhouse with a bunch of little birds inside.

Every question I answered led to a conversation of its own. "May! That's going to help a lot when you need to find a school." "Hey, my parents live around there!"

"Have you taken aerobics before? It's pretty serious, right? I don't know what it's like at other gyms, but I guess this place has a reputation for being kinda hard-core."

"Yeah, it's brutal. I swear, I thought my baby was gonna come."

Chirping filled the birdhouse, and I felt at ease.

Our Sunday afternoon conversation just kept going. Somebody got us on the topic of incontinence pads, and from there somebody else took the lead: she told us how when she visited her parents-in-law they told her she'd better have a boy, so on the train ride home she made an effigy out of the sleeve that her disposable chopsticks came in. Then someone else stepped up: she told us how she'd developed a serious craving for energy drinks, especially Dodecamin—so much that even her doctor was begging her to quit— and how she'd snuck out to a vending machine in the middle of a typhoon to get her daily fix. . . . This was a sight to behold. They were such a team: bump, set, spike.

At some point, one of them noticed a woman in a black top walking over to the vending machines by the entrance and said, "Hey, it's Ritsuko!" Everyone else in the group started waving. "Riiitsuko!" The woman in black waved back. She had her hair down and her clothes were different, so it took me a second to realize it, but she was our instructor. So that was her name ...

I listened to the others talk. Gachiko, who brought the doughnuts, and Kiku lived in the same building; their husbands worked at the same company. They were the ones who'd started the group. Hoya was going to give birth in the summer, which meant she had the longest way to go. Curly was due in May, the same month I was, but a little after me. Hosono was first up. She was due the month after next and was hell-bent on going out for yakiniku at least twice before then, since she wasn't going to be able to do anything like that once she'd had the baby. Her belly was already so big that I couldn't imagine it getting any bigger.

"Ugh! And my husband's telling me that even my face is getting rounder!"

"Hosono, you had such a small face to start with! Besides, after you give birth, you'll get a whole lot skinnier, whether you want to or not," said Chiharu, who already had two four-year-old girls. She was wearing a sweatshirt with a fox on it. I knew the shop where she got it. I'd been there myself—not that I bought anything. She was wearing a tight skirt, and her belly wasn't showing much yet. There was something so maternal about the giant backpack that she'd left hanging over the back of her chair, and the motley crew of cartoon characters on the keychains dangling from the zipper. The screen of her phone lit up beneath her creamy beige nails.

"Well, time to go. Gotta pick the girls up from gymnastics, and I guess I'd better grab a few things for dinner on the way."

"Oh, I've got to head out, too. I need to be home for a delivery."

Same here. Me too. Let's get going.

We all made our way out of the lounge. While we waited for the elevator, I spotted myself on the CCTV monitor: one of seven, sporting baby bumps of various sizes.

"Later, mommies!"

"See ya next week!"

When we left the gym, Hoya made a beeline for the closest station, and the others scattered shortly thereafter. Chiharu went into the Kinokuniya super-market, Hosono turned at the big intersection, and Curly said she was going to stop by her parents' house before going home. Gachiko and Kiku were heading in the same direction I was. It was a little overcast, but strangely warm for a February evening. The puddles left over from the rain we'd had the day before were flamingo pink.

I'd forgotten how the sidewalks around here were too narrow for three adults to walk side by side. We walked single file, only sometimes next to one anoth-er. Some disgruntled old man on a bicycle pulled up right behind Kiku, and Gachiko shouted, "Bike!" When she took the lead, I noticed how her bright yel-low sneakers really stood out against the concrete.

How long had it been since I'd walked anywhere, even around my own neighborhood, with other women like this? When I was a girl, we'd walk to school holding hands, or go over to each other's houses, or ride our bikes to the park. But that didn't last long. Soon we started going to the mall, or the movies, but we'd meet there, not go together. As an adult, I'm sure I did a fair amount of walking around the neighbor-hood with boyfriends, but when was the last time I did that with another woman? I think it was about the time I started my first job, when a coworker and I went together to pick up some drinks for a house party.

I called out to the two women walking in front of me.

"It must be nice for you guys, being pregnant at the same time and living in the same place."

"Yeah, it is. But company housing is the worst. If you don't follow the rules to a T when you're putting the trash out, you'll never hear the end of it. And the gossip, it's just insane."

"Yeah, I thought that kind of gossip was a thing of the past. Not even close! What about you, Shibata?" Gachiko asked. "What's your husband do?"

I stopped in my tracks. I could hear cicadas, even though it was only February.

"He's got . . . a normal office job," I said, almost jogging to catch up.

I bet he's cool, though. He's gotta be. He's probably got great style. Hey, does he look like anybody famous? Hmm, I dunno. It's hard to say if it's your own husband. . . . Yeah, totally. Makes sense. I dunno, Kiku, I really think your husband looks a lot like Pichon-kun. Come on, Gachiko, not that again! Pichon-kun? I know, right? Why would anybody know who that is? You know, he's the mascot for that air conditioner company. . . . You've definitely seen him before. Here, check it out.

Gachiko pulled out her phone to show me a cartoon character with a raindrop for a head. We were about to part ways.

"Well, I'm over here," I said at the bridge that leads to my apartment. They were heading toward the elementary school.

"Cool. See ya next time!"

We waved goodbye.

Once I was over the little bridge, I turned around. I could see the two of them walking slowly, leaning back a little. Even from this distance, Gachiko's neon sneakers stood out. The cicadas were really buzzing now—wherever they were.

When I got up to the third floor and walked through the door, I immediately sank to the floor. The cool, dark floor. The same floor as always. I didn't even change out of my clothes or turn on the light. I just lay there for a while, and around the time the white wallpaper started to blend into the shadow of the shoe cabinet, I reached over without getting up to grab my phone out of my bag and enter today's exercise into Baby-N-Me.

MOMMY AEROBICS. 50 MIN.

When I was doing the dishes after dinner, an invitation came through Line: MAMAS 2-B—THE MOMMY-ROBICS CLUB. I saw the group name on my screen, then went right back to cleaning. I took an early bath, did some stretches, watched a movie for a bit, then started reading a book, but I guess I couldn't stay focused. Some sort of wave with an invisible face, determined to disturb me, kept sweeping in, again and again, wiping away everything I'd read, and every time I tried to go back to reading, the wave came back again. I put down my book and thought about watering my pea sprouts, but then I remembered that I'd already changed the water in the morning. Too much water leads to root rot. Why overdo it?

Just a little before midnight, I got into bed and unlocked my phone. I set my alarm, then opened Line. MAMAS 2-B—THE MOMMYROBICS CLUB. The icon for the group was two girls who looked a lot alike, wearing identical yellow dresses. Chiharu's twins, for sure.

I didn't press JOIN or DECLINE. I just put my phone down and turned off the light.

Around the time that winter started to fade, I stopped watching movies on Amazon Prime. Not because there weren't any left to watch. There were tons, actually.

Through last week, I was watching movies pretty much every day. At first, I went through all the ones I'd missed when they were in theaters, or movies I'd heard about but hadn't seen—the so-called greats. I liked them all: *The Grand Budapest Hotel*, *Any Day Now*, *My Uncle*, *Antarctica*, *Amélie*. Once I'd gone through the titles that just came to mind, I moved on to the You May Also Likes. There was no end to the worlds that showed up on my screen: a diner in some cold, far-off place; an assassin taking in a young girl; pandemonium while a kid's parents are away. . . . At least I think that's what happened?

I dipped a toe into one world, then another.

I'd managed to see a whole lot of movies in less than a month. On the train, I started reading a blog called *The Best Movies You've Never Seen*, and I was surprised to find that I'd seen a good number of them.

But what surprised me most as I read the blog was how I couldn't remember much of anything that had happened in those worlds. These were movies I'd seen over the past few weeks. At first, I took notes on what I was watching, but I stopped before long. I couldn't keep up. That's why I can't even remember what I've watched anymore. It's a blur, most of the characters who have appeared on my screen simply passing through me. Most found happiness, some met tragedy, and a few more went on their way with knowing looks on their faces, as if they just might have figured it all out.

W HAT DO YOU WANT TO WATCH TODAY?

After a while, I started feeling like Prime was too demanding, so I found myself turning on the TV for the first time in ages. But who cares about artisanal croquettes that you have to line up to buy or B-list celebrities hamming it up on some quiz show? Everything on the screen was as flat as an old sock run over in the middle of the street.

The commentators on the news were no better. Or maybe they were pundits? I couldn't even tell. Before long, I turned off the TV again. I could just hear a voice coming through the thin wall. It was the next apartment over. At one point, the voice got a whole lot louder, as if someone had turned the dial on the radio all the way up, and then it went right back to what it had been. Even when the voice was really loud, I couldn't make out a single word.

Until last fall, there was a girl who was probably in college living next door. Her hair always looked nice, even when she just had it in a ponytail. Sometimes a guy who was probably her boyfriend came over, and when I passed them in the hall, they'd say hello in more or less perfect unison. But a little while ago, I saw somebody else opening that door: a woman, slightly older than I am. She had a face like an anteater. It had to be an entirely different person.

Since I stopped watching movies, I upped my visits to mommy aerobics. This week, I added Monday and Wednesday to the usual Tuesday, Thursday, Sunday. I guess I was there pretty much every day.

Weekday night classes were quiet. Almost nobody did any talking, so I could clear my mind and concentrate on what I was doing: stretches, steps, and exercises. "Yes! These are the muscles! That's it! These are the muscles you'll need when you push the baby out," the instructor said in a voice that really carried. I directed my thoughts to my belly and my thigh muscles. In the mirror, I lifted my arms higher than anyone. After class, I changed out of my exercise clothes, now covered in sweat, and drank some water. I plugged my numbers into Baby-N-Me, then walked home.

But on Sunday, things didn't follow the usual routine. Before we got started on our exercises, the studio was buzzing. No one said anything once the pace had picked up, but as soon as the cooldown was over, somebody said how she thought she was going to die from the workout, and then the whole room came alive again with conversation. Everybody was congratulating the women around them on having survived the ordeal. Except for maybe the woman in the neon-blue shirt. We drifted into the locker room, still chatting away, then found our way to the lounge.

Curly saw me coming over and scooted down.

"Hey, Sheeba! How was class?"

Last week, Hosono said, "Sheeba, you've got the prettiest hands I've ever seen." Since then, that's what the others have been calling me. I can't even remember the last time anybody had given me a new name like that.

Hosono asked Chiharu what she should bring when she goes to the hospital. She'd already started packing.

". . . Oh, and socks, for sure. Hospital rooms aren't exactly warm, and when you're walking around in slippers, your feet can get really cold. The thicker the better. Compression socks might be good. . . ."

In the middle of the table were the sweets that Gachiko had brought: bite-sized castellas. At home, her husband apparently gets mad at her for eating too much. As she complained, her meticulously drawn eyebrows came together in a frown.

"I mean, you should see the way he eats and drinks. It's so unfair. I never even get to go out drinking with friends anymore!"

"I dunno, Gachiko. At least your husband goes to the doctor with you. My husband couldn't care less. It's like he thinks the baby'll just show up all on its own. That's why I bought this. . . ."

Hoya pulled something out of her Marimekko backpack. Chiharu was mid-talk with Hosono, but her attention immediately shifted to Hoya.

"Oh hey, you got one!"

"Yeah, I felt like I had to. I wanted my husband to hear it. I know it's still kinda early, but . . ."

The pink device in her hand had the shape of a stethoscope. Well, it was a stethoscope.

"What is that?" I found myself asking. It looked kind of obscene.

"It's a stethoscope. You've never used one, Sheeba? You can listen to the baby's heartbeat with it. Yeah. That's a good idea. I think I'm gonna get one, too."

"But Chiharu, your husband doesn't need to be reminded that you're having a baby, does he?"

"It's not for him. I want one for me. It's just nice to be able to listen to your baby's heartbeat. I mean, I know that if I'm actually worried, I should go to the hospital, but what about late at night? I want his sisters to hear it, too. Like, hey, this is your baby brother."

"Wanna try? If you're okay doing it here."

"You sure?"

Chiharu took the stethoscope, rolled up her sweater, and placed the diaphragm on her belly. The old guys at the next table were looking at us, but she didn't seem to care.

"Can you hear it?"

"Hold up. Oh, yeah."

When Chiharu was finished, the others took turns. Gachiko tried it and said, "I can't hear a thing."

DIARY OF A VOID

Chiharu told her to try again, lower. Meanwhile, my side of the table was talking about parenting class. I listened as Curly complained about how her husband had said something moronic to one of the other women in their class, but soon the stethoscope made its way around. Hosono said she wanted to give it a try, then rolled up her thin sky-blue sweater, and there was her big round belly, popping out for all the world to see.

"Hmm . . . I think I can hear it?"

"Oh, you'll definitely hear a heartbeat."

"Yeah? That's not it, then. Hey, Sheeba, gimme a hand?"

Hosono wanted to cover her ears with both hands, so she gave me the stethoscope. I had no idea where I was supposed to hold it, so I slid it around. Her hand felt cold when she handed me the stethoscope, but her round belly was giving off a dazzling heat.

"Hey, there it is!"

In the moment that Hosono's gleeful voice echoed through the lounge, my hand brushed against her belly. I pulled it back right away, but the heat and smoothness didn't leave my fingers.

"I could totally hear it. It's so fast. Way faster than an adult's. Sheeba, you try," Hosono said as she pulled her sweater down. All I could do was say, "Not today," in a small voice.

When I got to the office the next morning, the section head called me over. Apparently there was a problem with the raw paper that had arrived at the factory the week before. He had me call the supplier to find out where things had gone wrong. The mistake was clearly theirs. I asked them to redeliver, then hung up. No big deal. But Higashinakano looked worriedly in my direction. As usual, he smelled like glue.

"Shibata, is everything okay?"

"What's that?"

"Um, sorry. That had to be a stressful call. I just thought you looked a little pale."

"I'm fine. It's nothing, really."

Nothing. It's true. And that's why I keep on making empty cores. Sometimes I wonder if the world really needs all these paper cores, but the orders keep coming in, so we keep making them. On and on the ribbon goes, never stopping. I was about to get started on something else when the supplier called back. They were out of stock, and it was going to take some time until they could deliver. I banged on the space bar over and over.

When I shot a glare back at Higashinakano, who was still looking at me even after I got off the phone, he apologized a few times, then turned back to look at his own screen.

It was March now, but the news was telling us that we'd be getting heavy snow starting in the afternoon. The entire Kanto area was going to have snow until early the next morning.

"I really want to get home before it gets too bad."

"What are the trains looking like over there?"

"That's nice. . . . At our office, it's business as usual."

Everybody was worried. I could hear them at their desks, in the hallway, on the phone with clients. Only they weren't *actually* worried. There was a hint of excitement in their voices. When I went to the stationery store to buy erasable pen refills, the guy behind the counter asked if it was snowing yet, and we both looked out the window. Not yet, I guess.

The snow started after I got back from lunch. At three, we got a company-wide email saying that anybody who was done with their work could head home. The guy at the desk opposite me started packing the second he saw it.

"Shibata, why don't you go home? You don't want to be on the trains when they start getting crowded."

"Thanks. I will. . . . As soon as I'm done with this."

"Well, don't stay too long." He shrugged on his maroon coat and left. The coat had a nice sheen to it. I bet it was velour.

It's time for me to get going. . . . Be careful. . . . The subway's getting really bad. . . . Silence. Within an hour, more than half of the office was gone. Others were sighing as they looked online for updates on trains. "Line's down," they'd say, loud enough for everyone to hear, even if it wasn't meant for anyone, then head down to the convenience store for meat buns or oden.

One desk over, Higashinakano was just staring at his computer, his back perfectly straight, as if he had a ruler stuck up the back of his shirt. The shirt he had on was bright yellow, which stood out even more now that the office was deserted. Did he pick that one out himself?

I'd finished what I was working on and was going to head home after printing out some documents, so I went over to the printers, then peeked out of the closest window. The sky was a dull gray, as if painted with layers of thin India ink. From the dim void overhead, countless snowflakes came swirling down in utter silence. Probably because it was so dark, I could see right into the offices in the building next to ours. I saw a short man in front of some steel shelves that went all the way up to the ceiling pulling out folders, then filing them away in slightly different places. From where I stood, every folder looked the same. It was like the man was engrossed in some game I couldn't hope to understand.

"The snow's looking pretty serious," said the guy using the printer next to mine.

"Yeah, I bet the trains are going to stop running. We'd better get home soon."

"Hey, Shibata," he said, speaking much quieter now. "Isn't it hard, sitting next to Higashinakano?"

He leaned in, practically whispering in my ear. Instinctively, I covered my belly with both hands.

"I wouldn't call it hard. . . ."

"Well, that's good to hear. He's so weird. The other day we were in the elevator together, and he banged his laptop against the wall, so I looked over, you know? He said, 'Sorry about the noise. . . .' But he kept saying it, pretty much shouting. I didn't say anything back, so he just started muttering to himself. There was somebody else in there with us, too. From another company. He was clearly freaked out. . . . I mean, what if something's really wrong with him?"

It looked like he wanted to keep talking, but I was done with my print job, so I went back to my desk and got ready to leave.

"I'm going home. Take care, Higashinakano."

"Thanks. I'll be leaving, too, as soon as I'm done with this. I've got to get this report ready for the section head. He said he needed it today—no ifs, ands, or buts."

Higashinakano pointed at the document tray on the section head's desk, then almost bowed at it. But when was the section head going to get around to reading that report? He'd gone home hours ago.

By the time I got to the station, the number of trains in operation had been reduced, but they were still running. Only rarely were trains stopping between stations. It was just a little more crowded than usual, and all the passengers were united by a common prayer: please don't let the train stop. At one point, a woman got her bag stuck in the door, and the riders around her helped free it without saying a word.

After a few stops, the seat in front of me opened up and I sat down. As hot air rushed up from under the seat, my mind went blank. "Tchuff tchuff tchuff tchuff tchuff tchuff tchuff. Boarding the train and heading north, they arrived in the Kingdom of the Snow Foxes." In a picture book that I loved when I was probably in kindergarten, a circus troupe got on a train and put on shows all around the world. They performed everywhere: a desert kingdom, a hidden forest world, a village of dwarves. Sometimes they didn't take the train but traveled by ship or camel. At night, they'd string up hammocks in their tent and go to sleep. That part never changed.

When I stepped onto the elevated platform at my station, the street below me was floating in a white haze. It was like a town I'd never seen before. Beneath the dim lights lining the street, fresh snow quickly undid the faint trails of footsteps that people had left behind.

At the supermarket, most of the shelves of perishables and canned goods had already been picked clean, leaving me unable to make the dinner that I'd been dreaming about while on the train. Figuring I'd just make do with whatever I had at home, I made my way toward the exit, but it was too much trouble to return the empty basket to the side opposite the exit, so I grabbed a container of high-end Greek yogurt that I'd never even considered buying before. I tried it after I finished the soup that I'd thrown together—and it really wasn't particularly good or bad.

Cold, damp air crept in through the gap around my window. I'd filled the bath with hot water, but the tub itself was freezing, so by the time I'd finished washing myself outside the tub, the water was lukewarm. My bath doesn't have a reheat function, so I stood under the shower and let hot water rain down on me, staying still and warming my body in the tub for a while, as if waiting for something to pass.

Layer after layer of night. Even after I changed into my pajamas and dried my hair, it was only 9:00 p.m. On TV, they talked nonstop about the snow. A lot of the train lines had shut down, apparently, and every channel was showing the crowded platforms at Shibuya Station, or the long lines of people waiting for taxis. It seemed like there had been snowslides, too, so the woman on-screen—wearing a flimsy-looking down coat—repeated over and over that no one should go outside unless absolutely necessary. Eventually, I turned off the TV.

On social media, everybody was talking about the snow, posting views from their windows, information about trains, pictures of snowmen their children had made. I got tired of it before long, so I started looking into washing machines, theater performances I'd talked about going to with friends, and a few other things that had been on my mind, but that didn't take very long, either. The internet's a great place for finding out about stuff you're kind of interested in, but it can't really help with the things you really want to know. It's even worse for things you don't know anything about.

I wiped the condensation from the window with my finger. The snow had really picked up. From a pitch-black sky with no moon and no stars, it fell constantly, floating down without purpose or agenda. It was accumulating everywhere—on the roads, the buildings, the gardens. I tried to keep my eyes fixed on a single flake as it fell all the way to the ground, but in the face of the flurries swirling all around, I quickly failed. Orange and yellow lights blurred across the river. Someone drew the curtains in the corner apartment in the complex opposite mine.

Everybody's the same in the snow, I thought.

That's why we're all home now. I mean, I'm sure some people are out—still at work, or waiting for a train, or maybe they were lucky enough to be on vacation in some other country—but most people are home, and not because they planned it that way. Sure, there are common holidays, New Year's or Obon, but on those days everybody goes out, or visits their families. People plan how to spend those holidays in advance, and I'm sure some people spend a lot of money and energy on those plans, more than I could ever imagine. But tonight's different. Nobody saw this coming, and now they're all stuck at home, eating dinner, watching TV. Maybe on their own, maybe with somebody else.

I looked around my room. A small, seven-mat room. Tweed gloves were popping out of the pocket of the Chesterfield coat that I'd left hanging by the door all winter. The guy I went out with in college had given them to me. We started dating soon after we met in class, then broke up over the summer the year we got jobs. I guess I didn't really like him, and that's why I could keep wearing them. I bet I wouldn't even notice if he walked past me on the street or at the station. The same goes for the guys who came after him, and the temps I found placements for at my old job, and the other students from college, and the classmates I used to share notes with in high school.

I wondered what all those people were doing under this snow. Maybe they were shivering in a cab they'd finally caught, or making or waiting for dinner, or staring out the window, commenting on the snow and sipping hot chocolate. Maybe that's what making a family is all about: creating an environment in which people make space for one another—maybe without even trying, just naturally, to make sure that nobody's forgotten.

I shut my curtains, then curled up on my armchair with my head on the armrest. The screen of my phone lit up. It was a newsletter from a shopping site that I hadn't used in ages, so I unlocked my phone to delete it, but instead ended up opening Baby-N-Me, as I did every night. This week's introduction popped up.

WEEK 29: YOUR BABY IS NOW THE SIZE OF: A BUTTERNUT SQUASH.

A butternut squash?! My voice jumped a good two octaves.

Maybe the person who writes these intros eats a lot of butternut squash? I don't. I mean, I've never bought one. Maybe they sell them at a real grocer or an upscale market, but isn't the whole idea of comparing the size of your baby to fruits or vegetables to make it easier to imagine? If that was the goal, I feel like they should have gone with something a little more commonplace, something that pregnant women and their partners in their twenties and thirties could relate to. I did some looking around online, and it turns out butternut squash is great in soup. Still, I can't imagine there are that many people out there making butternut squash soup! I mean, this is butternut squash we're talking about. There isn't even anything buttery or nutty about it. . . .

But, who knows, maybe some people find comfort in being told that their baby's the size of a butternut squash. I bet they do. Even if they only kinda know what it is.

I suddenly wanted something of my own, something to make space for. Even if it was just my own and no one else could even see it—something like a lie. And maybe if I could really hold on to that thing, a snowy night like tonight might become something else, something just a little different. I entered the day's meals and exercise into the app, and a melody like a hymn started to play.

The March snow kept falling, over the city and everyone in it.

WEEK 30

Where does it come from? Spring arrives wrapped in an air all its own. It's in the all-too-bright world seen from the train window, in the potted plants taking over the city's balconies, in the gleam of fresh white sneakers.

The arrival of Hosono's baby came as a surprise to the whole group. And probably to Hosono herself.

"The baby came on Monday! She wasn't due for another three weeks."

"Three weeks?!"

"I mean, it happens all the time. Hardly anybody's born on their actual due date."

Kiku had her phone out to show us the baby photos that Hosono had sent to her. Everybody joined in for a round of oh-my-god-what-a-cutie, but what they were actually interested in was Hosono's early delivery, and it didn't take long for the conversation to head back in that direction. Of course. Everybody here was going to have the same experience within the next six months. When it comes to having a baby, cuteness can't be everything.

"When I go into labor, I'm pretty sure my husband's gonna freak out," Gachiko said glumly. "Same here," Kiku said. "He's already covering his ass, saying he'll be there for the birth if he can make it, but he's got work, so . . ."

"When I had the twins, my husband came, but he couldn't handle it, and the midwife had to get him out of the way," Chiharu said, sighing as she brushed a little lint from the hem of her loose-fitting dress. No more tight skirts for her—but her sense of style was as impeccable as ever. Today's dress was from Scye.

"Hey, you're next, Sheeba," Gachiko said, handing me a bright pink cherry blossom doughnut.

"If I could get it over with, believe me, I would."

The real cherry blossoms were supposed to be in full bloom the last week of March.

As of last week, I've eased up on aerobics, and I got rid of Amazon Prime while I was at it. With the extra time I now had, I went to the dentist. Chiharu was telling me how it'd be impossible to take decent care of my teeth once the baby was here, at least for a while. My teeth are the only thing I'd never had a problem with, but apparently it's a lot easier to get cavities when you're pregnant, because your hormones are off. The dentist took one look inside my mouth and asked, "Do you think you can come in for regular visits for a little while?"

So I signed up for weekly cleanings—teeth scaling, too.

"Almost there, aren't you?" said an elderly woman in the waiting room. She had spectacularly white hair, like a narcissus that had bloomed just that morning. She must have seen what I was doing on my phone. With a knowing smile, she asked, "Is that Mercari?"

"Yeah. I'm doing some shopping for the baby. Why not go used, right? New baby clothes are just going to get dirty, and it's not like they're going to last that long anyway."

"That's the truth! They'll get dirty before you know it. That's what kids are best at."

Then the dentist called from inside. Apparently it was the woman's turn.

"Today's my final visit. Figured I might as well

give myself a nice filling. I don't care what anybody says, you've got to treat your teeth like royalty. Well, I'm so glad I could meet the two of you on my last visit."

The woman posed in a mint-green ensemble that was old-fashioned and yet somehow futuristically elegant, twirled around in slippers with the dentist's name written on them in Sharpie as if they were pointe shoes that she'd been wearing for years, then pranced inside.

Got to treat your teeth like royalty, I repeated. In that moment, my eyes met with one of the goldfish in the tank just beyond the sofa. I said it one more time, softly. The fish sought cover behind some water-weeds. Before it could disappear behind the swaying red tips of the plants, I edged closer to the tank and said it one last time: treat your teeth like royalty.

I closed Mercari, opened Baby-N-Me, and read the introduction for week thirty.

This is when the baby's hair and nails do a lot of growing. The baby still has very little body fat and is far slimmer than the newborns you always see in photos. It's also apparently the time when the baby starts shedding the lanugo covering its body, leaving its skin as smooth as a dolphin's. I read every line of the description out loud, adding a few thoughts of my own in the process. I let the words fill my eyes and ears.

And share them with the goldfish, while I'm at it.

"Shibata." When I heard my name called, I headed inside.

Today we were scaling my lower teeth. Strange—I didn't see the woman with the white hair again. Not in the hallway or in the waiting room.

I've always gotten sleepy as soon as it gets dark. It doesn't even need to be completely dark, so long as it's a little darker than it had been. In elementary school, whenever we finished with the morning assembly or outdoor exercises, I'd come inside, and while I was slipping back into my indoor shoes in the entryway, the world around me would just fade to black.

"Shibata . . . are you okay?"

Whenever I'd come to, I'd be in my inside shoes, getting ready for the next class or changing out of my gym clothes—except maybe that was only a dream, and I was still in the entryway, shoeless and asleep.

"Shibata . . . over here."

Yeah, I heard you. I turned to stare at Higashinakano—except it wasn't Higashinakano calling my name. It was the factory technician.

"Are you feeling okay? You look a little tired. Do you want to take a break? If you can handle it, we've got only one more stop to go. There's machinery inside, so watch your step."

"Thanks," I said and looked ahead, where Higashinakano was standing by a PVC strip curtain. His visitor's hard hat was too large for his head, and the mask he had on to keep the paper dust out was too big for his face. He was looking inside and tapping his foot. In an uncharacteristically restrained (if still excited) voice, he said, "Look, Shibata. This is where the magic happens."

"I know."

"Amazing . . . it's really moving."

Yeah, I know. But this time, I kept my answer to myself.

When I got to work in the morning, Higashinakano was arguing with one of the younger guys from sales. There was some kind of problem with a batch of film cores that Higashinakano had been in charge of, and apparently after delivery to the client's factory, some ended up crushed during the winding process. The guy from sales was raising his voice, asking Higashinakano what he was going to do to fix it, but Higashinakano was actually fighting back, saying he'd sent the specs to the client's factory before-hand and they hadn't said anything. Unable to watch the two of them squabble any longer, the section head intervened, telling both of them to visit our factory, meet with the head technician, and come up with a new plan. For some reason, I had to go with them, too. What a pain.

On the way to the factory, Higashinakano and the sales guy didn't speak at all. On the crowded train, when Higashinakano lost his balance and landed on the sales guy's foot, the sales guy stomped on Higashi-nakano's foot in retaliation. It was honestly sickening. Our factory was out in the suburbs, so at least there was some comfort to be found on the way by looking out the window at the rivers and terraced fields.

What we learned by coming to the factory was that both parties were at fault. The sales guy was incredulous. He told the technician to make sure the units were redelivered within the next couple of days, then stormed out, saying he had another meeting to get to. Higashinakano couldn't believe he'd messed up. He apologized over and over. He wouldn't stop until the technician told him to snap out of it. After that, we checked all the details, and once we'd wrapped up, the technician asked if we wanted a tour of the floor. When we visited the factory like this, we didn't usually have the time to look around. The unexpected invitation put even Higashinakano in a good mood, and once they'd handed us our jumpsuits, masks, and hard hats, he could hardly contain himself. He was just like a kid on a field trip.

The factory floor was as sleepy as ever. In a building resembling an elementary school gym, there were maybe ten people in discolored jumpsuits in varying shades of green, working in silence like life-sized figurines. On the wall was a poster with NO I IN TEAM written in giant letters, and beside it was a timetable for the shuttle bus that ran between the factory and the station.

Higashinakano couldn't stop looking at the machinery set up by the entrance, so I left him there and headed inside, making sure to avoid the toolboxes by my feet. The paint on the machines was chipping in places, and a thick layer of dust had collected on the metal. I touched one of the brown ribbons and watched it sink beneath my fingertips. Among the high-pitched scratches and screeches, I heard a little squeak that sounded like a rusty swing.

"Here we go!"

The technician waved us back a little. Two men pointed at something and called out to each other. Then there was a low rumble.

Slowly, the ribbons started moving, trembling ever so slightly, as if pushed forward by a giant invisible hand. There really wasn't much to it. No bright color, no pattern to catch the eye. They just move on, get glued, then pass over a series of rollers before getting wound up in spirals. That's all. There was a single beam of light spilling in through a small skylight, falling over the ribbons. It wasn't so different from film running through a projector, except it conjured no beautiful drama, no astonishing action. It just kept going—rolling on and on.

Somebody save me, I thought to myself. I remembered how I always used to hope to find rejects on trips to factories. A malformed seat belt, maybe, or a book with miscut pages. That was what I wanted to see. Unexpected cracks in a giant system that seemed so unassailable. But big factories like this one always had the newest machines, and put money and manpower into what they did, meaning an oddity was a very rare thing to come by. No—at this factory, there wasn't even the possibility of anything going wrong. A reject was simply too much to ask for.

Long ribbons of paper getting pulled along, then rolled up. Just that, nothing else. As long as the power didn't cut out and the machinery kept running, there wasn't even a chance of a mishap. The pieces just kept going, nothing there to pique my interest. I could see why the others who had come to the factory for training were bored out of their minds.

But it was kind of like a spell. The ribbon never stopped rolling. It just kept moving, and once it was in motion, nothing was going to stop it. If somebody stuck a finger in, it would get sliced clean off. On and on each ribbon went, drawing the next ribbon forward, creating layer after layer. There was nothing here dazzling enough to describe as magic. No cutting-edge technology. The spell was in the obsession, the relentless intensity. Words summoning more words, making space for a new story to come into the world. Solemnly, modestly, reverently. And inside the core a void. Ready for whatever story was going to fill it.

The spell ran on, making its way through the dim light of the factory. On and on and on . . .

As the rolled-up ribbons moved on, they were sliced into sections and fitted with clasps or special tops and bottoms when necessary. The smaller cores could end up used in plastic wrap or canisters for tea, while the bigger ones were likely destined for some more industrial purpose. There truly must be countless uses in the world for paper cores. That's why the ribbon never stops. Here in this sleepy factory.

Once we'd returned our jumpsuits and left the factory, the air was filled with light and sound. Higashinakano was on the phone. It was a long ride from the factory to the station, and other than the employee shuttle that we'd taken here, there was no way back except by taxi. When I sat on the bench in front of the factory, I could smell nothing but earth all around me. My black jacket was absorbing the heat, so I took it off and rolled up the sleeves of my dress. In the field across the wide road, there was a woman with a headscarf planting something.

"I'm glad we got a chance to see the factory," Higashinakano said softly as he came back.

"Me too," I said as I took a sip of vegetable juice. Its container was apparently made here, at this factory.

When we were done with the tour, our host told us about all the latest products and the costs for various custom pieces, then gave us loads of samples to take back to HQ. "And tell the others at the office to come and visit, too," he added as we shook hands and said goodbye.

"But, Shibata, all the narrow spaces and stairs must have been really hard on you. . . . You're due in May, right? So it's about the time when you need to start seeing the doctor a whole lot more. . . ."

"It is. . . . But why do you know so much about childbirth?"

Higashinakano's glasses caught the light of the sun. His lenses were so much thicker than the kind you usually see these days.

"My wife and I can't have children, but we were trying for a while. We gave a lot of thought to what it would be like to have a baby, and how amazing it would be to raise a child together."

You're married! I wanted to say, but the words wouldn't come. I was beyond shocked.

"So when I heard you were pregnant, I thought, 'Good for her.' I mean, I'm sure it's a lot for you. . . . And I know you're on your own. Sorry, I shouldn't say anything. But I told my wife all about you. I told her that you're having your baby on your own, but that you always make it look so easy. Anyway, we gave up trying. Once we made up our minds, things got a lot easier for us, but . . . we both still wish we could."

Higashinakano kept talking. He told me how surprised he was by the cost of IVF treatment, how the constant tests and pills really took a toll on his wife, how they got into fights every time he said anything about calling it off, how she managed to get pregnant once, but miscarried, and how they had never told their parents about the treatment. He spoke with an ease that I'd never seen from him at work. He met his wife at school. They were in choir together. Maybe that bright yellow shirt he was wearing when it was snowing was something she'd picked out for him. I started wondering what kinds of feelings must have been passing through him when he wrote down that list of names to go with Shibata.

"I'm sorry, maybe that's too much information? Th-thanks for coming today."

"Not at all. I was happy to see the factory again after so long."

"I know I messed up and everything, but . . . didn't they look like pretty good cores to you? Even if they were a little off. . . ."

Higashinakano pulled a misshapen paper core out of his backpack. The technician had given him one that had been produced to the wrong specs—as a kind of souvenir. Under the late March sun, the light gray core looked so fragile, but it was hardly calling out for sympathy.

I had no idea what to say. All I could think was how mad the sales guy would be if he'd heard this conversation.

In the distance, I saw a flicker of light among the houses. A car. Probably the taxi that Higashinakano had called.

"You wanna touch my belly?"

"Oh, I couldn't. . . . This is a really important time for your baby," Higashinakano said as he pulled out a terry-cloth handkerchief. He quickly wiped his hands with it, rubbed them together, then put the handkerchief away before pulling it out again and repeating the cycle. He made no motion toward my belly.

As the taxi approached, I could see a stuffed seal on the dashboard. "Come on," I said, thrusting out my belly. "Our ride's coming."

"Okay, if . . . if you're sure."

Higashinakano touched my belly with his chapped, childishly small hand. It felt warm. I was no longer padding my shirts.

"Wow! What a kick! Your baby's really in there!"

There was a tremor in his voice. The seal was getting closer. Getting bigger by the second. Its plastic eyes starting to shine.

The baby's been kicking so much more lately.

When the people on the talk show started discussing the celebrity scandal that had been all over the news the past few days, I went out onto the balcony to hang the laundry. I could feel a mild breeze clinging to my cheeks and my calves. The neat rows of cherry trees across the river were nearly bare by now, but the trees behind the shrine were supposed to be in full bloom this week. "Cherry blossoms are so pretty . . . but the best thing about them is that they don't smell," Hoya said last week on the walk back from aerobics. "If they smelled half as strong as sweet olive blossoms, nobody would ever want to drink under them."

Maybe I should go and see the cherry blossoms, I thought as I clipped my socks to the plastic drying hanger. I can make some lunch with whatever I have in the fridge—as soon as I finish with the laundry and cleaning the bathroom. Who knew maternity leave was going to be so much work?

I started maternity leave on April 1. I was supposed to be at work for one more week, but I had paid time off left over, and HR recommended I get an early start. On my last day in the office, Higashinakano gave me a string of paper cranes. I spent my first day of leave the way I'd spend any other day off: cleaning up around the house. But that night it hit me. This was no ordinary day off.

The next day, after a little morning cleaning, I headed out for lunch. I walked to a Chinese restaurant where I'd eaten once before. The food was great, but it was too far from the train station, so I hadn't been back. When I got there, it was just after noon, but there were no office workers in sight. At one of the tables, an older couple sat with impeccable posture as they slurped their noodles, while someone else in their sixties—I couldn't tell whether it was a man or a woman—sat at the counter drinking beer and eating zha cai. I had the mapo tofu, and it was amazing. I've always liked Sichuan better than chili pepper. A little later, I ordered a nonalcoholic beer.

I thought about what was ahead of me: childbirth and everything that would follow. There was so much to be done. I'd finally signed up for childbirth classes the night before. Where I live, you're eligible for just the first thirty-six weeks. I was cutting it close.

Since last month, I'd put on a lot of weight. When I stepped onto the scale in the locker room before aerobics, I found that I'd been gaining a little over a pound a week for the past three weeks or so. Going to see the cherry blossoms wasn't just for fun. It was something I had to do to stay in shape. Baby-N-Me recommended walking, too—and also told me to watch out for constipation. I put on a dress I'd bought from Zara (it wasn't a maternity dress, but it was loose fitting), stepped into my sneakers, and left the house.

Recently, every day has been just as beautiful as the one before. When I go outside, everything gives off so much light. The river's full of all kinds of life. The water's dazzling, and I turn around toward the steep slope behind my building to find a sky almost too blue to believe. Against the sky, a profusion of cherry blossoms.

After I had my lunch while looking up at the cherry blossoms behind the shrine, I went to the dentist. Now that I was on leave, I could take any appointment, any time of day. And the dentist told me he could do everything I needed to have done before my due date.

As I was waiting to pay, a woman who was obviously pregnant came in, holding the hand of a little girl, and stepped listlessly into a pair of slippers. Our eyes met. Neither of us said a word, but we exchanged something powerful—as if we were both equipped with that infrared function that cell phones used to have—and then I left. The little girl was gripping the woman's hand, staring straight at my belly as I walked out.

In the evening, the wind came blowing in through the open window. I stepped out onto the balcony to bring in the laundry. The sky had turned violet, and the warmth of the day had been mercilessly forgotten—the coolness of the air gave me goosebumps. Across the river, along the tree-lined road, I could see a group of boys with backpacks way too bulky for their scrawny bodies. There were six or seven of them in all, and they had to be in first or second grade. I hadn't seen any kids their age in so long that I was beginning to wonder if there were any of them left.

I had no idea what the boys were saying, but it was

like nothing in the world could have been more inter-
esting to them. As they spoke, they passed single file
by the flowerbeds, then broke into different forma-
tions, changing shape like an amoeba. One of the
boys was wearing shorts.

It was always like that in elementary school. There
was one kid in every class who was always wearing
shorts, even on the coldest day of the year. And it was
always one kid, exactly one. Those kids were never
put in the same class—I guess the teachers made sure
of that. I wonder what happened to those kids. Are
they all grown up now and wearing pants? I can't
imagine how sad they must have been the first time
they had to put on a pair of actual pants.

"Yamada did it! Yamada did it!"

When the boys were just across from my balcony,
that's what I heard, clear as day. As they kept walking,
a few of the others joined in. *Yamada did it! Yamada
did it!*

Soon the voices grew louder, chanting in unison.
Yamada did it! Yamada did it!

The chant started to swell, becoming a giant wave.
I couldn't pull myself away. The sky was changing
color like a banana going bad, the clouds breaking
apart one after another and drifting on.

But by the time the boys reached the intersection, the wave had died down. Their voices had returned to normal as they turned the corner and vanished from view. I felt the tension leave my shoulders, but I kept my eyes on that scene for a while. I wondered which one Yamada was, and what he'd done. Maybe he wasn't even one of them—not that I had any way of knowing. At least Yamada was real to them, even if only in their heads.

Eventually I realized I was shivering. In my sandals, my toes were turning purple.

"Sorry, I bet you're feeling cold, too," I said to my belly, then stepped back inside, laundry in my arms.

Whoa, it moved.

The words spilled out of my mouth before I'd even realized what I was saying. Stepping onto the bus, I almost got my finger caught in my umbrella as I pulled it shut.

"Are you okay?" the bus driver asked. "Need a hand?"

"Thanks, I'm fine," I said as I made my way up to the Suica reader. Two hundred ten yen. The fare for one adult. I can still ride the bus for the price of one, at least for a little longer.

The driver told us to find something to hold on to, and as the bus shuddered into motion, I fell back into one of the priority seats. Outside the window, in the light rain, a hazy white scene passed by. Little feet kept kicking inside of me. Those sweet little feet.

The hardest part of the checkup came before I even saw the doctor. Once I got to the hospital that I'd found online, I told the woman behind the counter that it was my first visit, and she launched into a lecture in a shrill voice, telling me how absolutely critical it was for expectant mothers to see a doctor if they wanted to bring their baby safely to term. And she was right. I stood there listening, head lowered, until an older orderly stopped her and led me through the waiting room.

The doctor was in a room at the far end of the hall, sitting in a velvet-covered chair. His eyes looked like a pair of marbles behind his glasses, so clear you could see right through them. His close-cropped hair had lost its color. Sitting in front of his old-fashioned medicine cabinet, he seemed more like a librarian than an obstetrician. He was nice to me, maybe because he knew it was my first visit. Or maybe he didn't know what to do with a woman who had waited until her thirty-sixth week to see a doctor.

As soon as I walked in, he took one look at my belly and said, "You're well on your way, aren't you?"

He asked if this was going to be my first baby, then we just spoke for a little while. He started the actual exam only after telling me how his Yorkshire terrier was always peeing on his bed.

For the ultrasound, the doctor turned off the lights,

asked me to lie down on the examination table, and then slathered my belly with some cold gel before pressing the probe against it. Although I couldn't see the monitor from where I lay, I could see a bluish flicker taking over the darkness of the room.

"That's strange," the doctor said, then went silent. Nothing else. I waited for him to explain. "The image is a little fuzzy," he said, then pulled out his laser pointer.

"See? This is your baby. Kicking away. The picture of a healthy baby."

I turned my head to see, and there it was. This little being in the shape of a person. I widened my eyes and concentrated all my thoughts on my belly.

"That's . . . the baby?"

"Sure is. *Your* baby."

The doctor pointed at the image on the screen. All I saw was a sandstorm, bits of dust blowing all over the place. Here's the head, the doctor said. Well, the back of the head. Over here's the belly. A nice little belly. Here's the butt. And the feet. And see over here? These are the hands.

I listened, carefully taking in each word the doctor said.

Head.

Belly.

Butt.

Feet.

Hands.

I muttered each word to myself—almost as if they were foreign words I'd never pronounced before. The shape on the screen became more solid before my eyes. It was as if a storm that had enveloped everything all night long had finally settled, revealing a secret flower garden that had been waiting for this moment.

"Hey, did you see that? Your baby's really moving! Um, are you okay?"

Sorry, I'm sorry. . . . I tried to respond, but no words came.

There was a baby there. It had a place in the world. It had taken its own form, a human form. Out of nothing.

"Don't worry, Shibata. Plenty of moms cry when they see their babies for the first time. There's a box of tissues, if you want. . . ."

Thank you, I said, then gave my nose a good strong blow, all the while keeping my thoughts focused on the screen. A nurse came in with another box of tissues. On the side were a bunch of little chicks. Baby birds walking in a line.

The doctor kept toying with the knobs below the monitor.

"Hmm. Well, the rest of the image is clear, but the face is still a blur. Strange. Hold on a minute, okay? I'm pretty sure I can fix this. . . ."

"It's okay, thanks. Let's stop here. I guess I wasn't prepared. . . ."

"Stop here? Are you sure?"

I'll do everything I can to be ready next time, I said, then I sat up. I used a towelette to wipe the gel off my belly, then left the exam room.

I t wasn't the rumble of the bus as it started to move, and it wasn't an earthquake. There was something inside me, moving. The world around me was blurry with raindrops, but I could still see shop signs and the tops of people's heads as they drifted by.

I pulled out my notebook and looked at the photo that the doctor had given me. Before I'd left the hospital, I was at the counter, finding out about the checkups and how much they would cost, when the doctor hurried out of his office with a picture in his hand. The pale light inside my belly. Tiny hands reaching out to grab something. Little feet eager to leave their mark.

So this is the price to pay. For creating another person, for spinning words.

I was in pain. Serious pain. There was something inside me, pushing against my intestines, pressing against my lungs, messing with my bones. I doubled over and stroked my arm again and again through my dress.

"Um, you okay?" the older man in the priority seat next to mine asked. I was covered in a greasy sweat, unable to do anything but nod.

WEEK 37

WEEK 37: YOUR BABY IS NOW THE SIZE OF: A BUN-
DLE OF SPINACH.

I lifted my eyes from the screen and glanced over
at my fridge. Oh yeah. I went with komatsuna this
time. The spinach was too expensive. I flopped down
on my armchair. My stomach was empty, but there
was no way I could bring myself to prepare a meal.
Just the thought of steamed vegetables fogging up the
little kitchen window or the smell of meat cooking
was enough to make me want to throw up.

The nausea hasn't gone away—and neither has the
pain. The baby's been moving around for some time
now, and sometimes I feel a heaviness around my hips,
but ever since my last visit to the doctor, the kicking
has gotten even stronger. The pain is entirely different now: an intense pressure on my organs that makes
me feel like I can't breathe. Sometimes it's too painful
to move.

The baby seems entirely indifferent to my will. When I try to sleep, he starts kicking. Then, when it seems like he's finally done, he launches into a somersault. When he presses against my bladder or my cervix, the pain is so sharp that I feel like I'm being crushed from the inside. When I had Amazon Prime, I saw a scene in a mob movie where they cut open a guy's chest—no anesthetic—and pulled out his beating heart. Now I know: that kind of torture isn't just in the movies. I'm supposed to have another appointment at the hospital tomorrow, but I'm not sure I'll be able to get on the bus and make the trip. Inside of me, there's another person, with a form all his own, moving around as he pleases. It's like my own body has become foreign to me.

Did you ever feel that way? I asked Chiharu one day when I'd barely managed to make it to the gym.

"For me, morning sickness was the worst. But there are definitely people who have all kinds of problems later on. Hey, Sheeba, watch out for the baby blues."

Chiharu told me how a lot of people get depressed after giving birth, then pulled out her phone to show me a city-run website with a list of resources.

"There are places in town you can go for help. I

mean, you can always come to me, but there are some things that are hard to share with friends, right? Things you don't want to say."

I could see an ear cuff peeping out from her perfect-as-ever bob.

I groaned as the baby landed a perfectly executed dropkick on my bladder. I couldn't stay seated any longer, so I started pacing around the room. If it were an option, I would have taken something for the pain, but all I had at home was Loxonin, and I wasn't supposed to have that during my final twelve weeks.

Maybe it had burned out. As I stepped outside, I could see a red star hanging low in the sky to the south. When I reached the landing, I checked to see if it was still there, and then headed downstairs. I cut through the bike lot and headed onto the street behind the building. According to my phone, it was a little after eleven thirty at night.

A few hours ago, I was feeling drained, as usual, so I figured I might as well head to bed and get some rest, but the sudden onslaught of kicks ruined any chance of sleep, so I slipped into my sandals and went outside. I walked along the river, making my way toward the hill. I was out of breath before I could reach the top, but I kept climbing, refusing to accept that the asthmatic wheezing I could hear was actually coming from me. Through my cotton pajama pants, I could feel the night air on my skin.

Once I made it to the top of the hill and the road leveled out, I headed down a residential street. It was the same area I'd seen that pregnant woman doubled over the first time I walked home from work. But I'd never been here so late at night before. There wasn't anybody around—only the occasional vending machine standing by the side of the road, glowing with a life of its own.

As I turned a corner, I froze. There was something down the road. Someone? They were standing by a bulletin board across from a huge house that had to belong to some wealthy family, but moving: up and down, back and forth, rhythmically. What is it with all the strange people in this neighborhood? I felt a kick. *Keep going.* One kick, then another, nudging me forward. Slowly, I drew closer.

The person was rocking.

Every movement was so small—every bend of the knees, every sway of the arms—but they came together to form a kind of dance. The dancer was moving to a song that no one else could hear. Maybe it was some kind of ritual. I'd never seen a real rain dance before, but that was what it looked like to me.

The dancer seemed tired. Beyond tired. When they pulled one hand away from the big bundle at their chest, they bent forward awkwardly, then thumped their back and shoulders with the free hand. Maybe the dance was supposed to help with stiffness? Every now and then, the dancer rubbed their eyes, then quickly returned to the same stance as before—rocking, swaying, as if putting a baby to sleep.

Then they turned to me. A slender white face emerged from the dark.

"Sheeba? That you?"

It was a voice that should have sounded familiar—but tinged with the kind of hoarseness that comes from a lingering cold. Still, there was no mistaking it. It could have been her accent, or maybe it was her pronunciation, but no one else called me "Sheeba" that way. Of course, I remembered, she was the one who'd given me that name in the first place.

"Hosono? How are you doing? I mean, what are you doing out here?"

"It *is* you. Going for a walk? This late at night? Good for you."

Hosono smiled, and as she did, her face—which had been so small to begin with—became even smaller, so small it had nothing left to give.

"It's been a while, huh? How are you doing? How is everybody? I'm pretty sure I saw Curly the other day on the bus. How's Gachiko? Still snacking?"

"Uh-huh, always snacking on something. The other day she put away a whole box of rusks."

"I bet," Hosono said, then she started to laugh but ended up choking. She was coughing so violently that I was sure her tiny back was about to burst open. Even as she coughed, Hosono didn't stop rocking. To an indiscernible rhythm, she kept moving, up and down, along with a baby carrier that kind of looked like a piece of armor. Her socks, after a valiant effort to cling to her nonexistent calves, finally surrendered and fell to her ankles. Hosono didn't seem to mind.

"Sorry, that can't sound good. Hey, Sheeba, aren't you due pretty soon? How are you feeling? I know it's not an easy time."

"Hosono . . ."

"Yeah?"

"Congrats. You're a mom."

Yeah, thanks, Hosono said. I thought I saw something almost invisible flooding her eyes—and, in that same moment, I felt a dull pain in my lower back. I doubled over and held my breath. When I looked up again, Hosono was looking down, her face now hidden. So was the little face in the baby carrier.

"That was in March, right?"

"Uh-huh."

"Wow. You really did it. She's a girl, right? Kiku had photos and was showing them to everyone. She's a real cutie."

"Thanks, thanks."

Hosono was still swaying. She didn't look up, but at one point she moved one of her hands. I'd never stared at Hosono for so long. Every single thing about her was thin: her skinny arms, her knobby wrists, everything. She looked so much more like a teenage girl than a woman who'd just had a baby. I had to wonder what Hosono was like when she was in school.

The downstairs lights went off in the big house. It was already April, but it was still getting chilly at night. I rubbed my legs together. I wished I'd put on some socks before leaving the house.

"Hey, it's almost midnight. I was just walking around, but what are you doing out? Aren't you cold? I bet your husband's worried about you."

"Yeah."

"Hosono?"

Her chest was slowly rising and falling. Over and over. I could hear something like leaking air. Then I caught a glimpse of the tiny face at her chest—cheeks that looked smoother and softer than fresh cream. The baby slept between Hosono's chest and arms, with a look on her face like she lived in a world free of pain and sadness.

"Everything's great, just as long as I keep holding her like this."

When the upstairs lights went off in the big house, Hosono spoke. She was so quiet—like we were a couple of on-duty librarians. She was still rocking, never stopping, as if even a momentary pause would result in some disaster.

"She's so cute and wonderful. So precious. It's true, it's all true. Babies are so cute."

"They really are."

"They really are! That's what everybody says."

She held her daughter tight in her arms and looked up. In the darkness of spring, something had burst open.

"Everybody says so. 'You must be so happy,' 'You're

so lucky,' 'She has your eyes.' But she doesn't! She's always crying! I can't even get a good look at her face. Well, when I was with my parents, and my mom was holding her, I kind of thought she looked like me. But since we came home? Nothing but crying. She's always crying. She sleeps sometimes. Just for short stretches, but she sleeps. And that's when I need to wash her bottles. They need time to dry. Then I have to do the chores. How does anybody keep this up? Are they superhuman or what? Am I supposed to hang the piles of laundry and do all the cleaning while carrying this kid the whole time? The second I put her down on the bed, she starts screaming. I swear, it's like she's got a button on her back. What's your problem with gravity? Why do you hate lying down so much? Did somebody murder you in your sleep in a past life? Anyway, it's fine. It's not Yuri's fault. Oh, that's her name. Yuri. She's a part of me, another me. And, sure, I know it's not going to last forever. She really is precious, though. The real problem's my husband. What good is he? At night, when Yuri's crying, he gets all pissed off about how he has to go to work in the morning. Actually, I wish he'd get pissed off more. He always tries to hold it in. And that really pisses me off. I can tell how mad he is, but he acts like he's so understanding. Yeah right. I mean, if you understand, why don't you do anything to help out on weekends? Why do I have to bring Yuri outside in the middle of the night like this? And don't you dare sigh at me. Not that long, stupid sigh again. Don't act like you're doing a great job just because you managed to get her to fall asleep once. You say you're gonna buy her something really cute from Baby Depot, so I ask you to pick up some sweat pads for me while you're there, and then you come back all proud about the outfit you got her, even though it's way, way, way too big. . . . And what about the sweat pads I needed? Ugh! What I wouldn't give to sleep for, like, a solid thirty minutes!"

A window in the building behind us slammed shut. Then another. The message was loud and clear. Hosono seemed wholly unfazed by it. What stopped her from going on was the sweet little voice at her chest.

Feh, feh . . .

Hosono didn't move at all. Neither did I. Under the fluorescent light, her face lost color. I stared silently at her dark green baby carrier. I felt a tension inside my belly.

Feh, feh, feh . . .

Once the baby's breathing had settled, Hosono let out a sigh, then started rocking again. It seemed like hours had passed since I left my apartment.

"That was a close one."

That was all she said, and then she went silent. I didn't say anything, either. I had no idea what to say, but I couldn't imagine saying, "It's getting pretty late—I better get home." It was obvious that neither of us had anywhere else to go.

"But your husband sounded so nice."

In my head, I replayed the conversations we'd had in the lounge.

"Didn't he go to the doctor with you? Wasn't he helping around the house when you had morning sickness?"

Holding her daughter with one arm, Hosono used her other hand to scratch her cheek. Two, maybe three times. It didn't seem like she was trying to scratch an itch. I looked at her fingers, unable to believe how bony they were.

"Sure, he helps and all, but he's still basically a stranger."

"A stranger?"

"Yeah, his part was simple, right? All he had to do

was ejaculate. After that, my body took care of the rest. I got bigger, I threw up, sometimes I couldn't even move. Sure, sometimes he'd notice and offer support. And, yeah, he cried when Yuri was born, but as far as he's concerned, he just came inside me, then months later here was this baby girl. I know women are the only ones who can give birth, but once the baby's born, why the hell should our roles be so different? Breastfeeding, I get, but what about everything else? Don't tell me you need more time to figure out how to be a dad. Like, what have you been doing for the last nine months? Don't just sit there and watch. This isn't a field trip! You say you've got work, but what about me? I've got work, too! Well, I did. I know it paid nothing compared to what you make. . . . Anyway, isn't that what paternity leave is for? I'm not saying take it right now, but did it occur to you that maybe I could work and you could stay at home? Did it even occur to you? Why should I act so grateful just because you changed your daughter's diaper one time? Has it ever crossed your mind that maybe I'm worn out? Maybe it has, but, what, you think that's just part of being a mom? Do you think he knows how it feels, Sheeba? Do you think he gets it? Even though he's maybe eight inches away, blissfully asleep, he's more of a stranger than some random politician I've never met or some stray dog somewhere in Brazil. I feel more alone with him than I do when I'm on my own."

My attempt at making her feel better had backfired. Hosono's anger had exploded like fireworks; now it was burning on like a signal fire. Out of the corner of my eye, I saw someone step out onto the balcony across the way and look at us, but we didn't mind. Then I heard the words "I get it" spill out of my mouth.

I know that Hosono isn't the only one who feels this way. Chiharu must have felt that same kind of anger. And maybe something similar awaits Hoya and Gachiko. Maybe even my mom felt that way. My mom who can't help but dip her spoon into my ice cream.

As Hosono went on, I looked up and found that same star in the sky. The red one I'd seen when I left my apartment. There it was, hanging over a cluster of high-rises.

Then, for just a second, the light went out.

Wondering if my eyes were playing tricks on me, I opened them wide. There it was. Of course it was still there. Stars don't just disappear. But as I trained my eye on the red dot, it vanished again, then quickly reappeared. I was pretty sure the star was moving.

It was blinking. Regularly. *Daah, daaah*. All the while moving at a set speed. Then I remembered the airport over there, on the other side of the high-rises. The red lights had to belong to planes landing and taking off.

"Actually, Hosono. Sorry, but I don't get it."

She raised her eyebrows. Her face was as small as ever. I'd always been so envious. I had to wonder how Hosono's husband looked at her every day—at her perfectly placed eyes, nose, mouth.

"And your husband probably gets it even less. Maybe he's trying. Maybe he's not. And I know what you mean about him sighing and everything, and he should definitely be there for you and the baby, but ..."

I kept going. As I spoke, I tried to remember the first time I'd come down this street. I was a little tired then. Yeah, I was on my way back from work. It was the first time I decided to walk home, figuring that I had put on some weight and could probably stand to walk a station or two. When was that?

"I bet the others would get it, especially Chiharu. She said it was hard with the twins. The others would sympathize, too. But, really, no one else is you."

That's right. It was winter then. I'm pretty sure I

had my coat on. I'd just gotten through my first trimester, so it had to be December. My belly was getting gradually bigger. I was starting to get used to
being pregnant.

"I've been reading a lot of childbirth and pregnancy blogs lately. Don't you think it's weird how in
an age of cryptocurrency and telework, childbirth—
something experienced by pretty much half the
world's population—is still so hard and so painful?
Breastfeeding, giving the baby all you've got, never
getting a half hour to just sleep . . ."

After I got pregnant and I started coming home
on time, it was a real shock to leave the office so early.
But it wasn't actually early at all. That's why it's called
"on time." Of course it was okay to leave. I was so surprised to see how crowded the trains were just a little
after five. And I was even more surprised to discover
that nobody else seemed to think there was anything
special about that.

"And there are a lot of people—husbands, parents-
in-law, even your own parents—who say horrible things
that make you want to say, 'Fine, let's trade places.'
But they can't. They can never take your place. They
can't even understand you. Because they're not you. I

mean, I'm standing right here with you, Hosono, and there's no way for me to really get how depleted you are, how exhausted."

December. That end-of-year party was such a waste of money. I've felt this way ever since I started living on my own, but the first step toward responsible spending is to avoid going out drinking, especially when you don't even want to go. It's not only a waste of time and money, but you have to listen to all these stupid people going on and on. Then, when they're finally done talking about themselves, they'll start asking you all these questions about your private life? No thanks.

"I'm sure it happened a bunch of times. While you and Curly and the others were throwing up, dealing with morning sickness, cooking dinner for your husbands even though you were totally drained, fighting back tears while you chopped up some pork or bell peppers, I was at home enjoying a slice of cake. I'm not saying I want everybody to be miserable. Of course I don't. I don't want that for anybody, and I definitely don't want it for myself."

But why do I have to deal with these people who try to act like they care about me or my pregnancy while they ask the most inane, prying questions? Why is it up to me to produce answers that please them? And why is the way home so much darker and colder on nights like that?

More than that, why is my apartment so dark when I come home alone from aerobics, after talking with the others about nothing in particular, snacking on whatever sweets are spread out on the table?

"I'm so alone. I'm sorry—this has nothing to do with how hard things are for you, Hosono. But I'm always so alone. I guess I should be used to it by now. That's the way it is from the moment we come into this world, but I'm still not used to it—how alone we all are."

As I spoke, I heard my voice break for the first time in a long while. The lights in the apartment behind Hosono went out. It was the kind of red-brick building you don't see much of these days.

When I was growing up, we lived in an apartment building where my dad's company had a number of units. It was a gloomy building at the farthest end of the school district, with a roof of blue fish-scale tiles. The building's caretaker was an old woman who lived on her own. She had a habit of muttering to herself, and her tangled hair looked just like a bird's nest—so everybody called her the Witch.

The Witch was always in a terrible mood, but she really couldn't stand it when someone tried to sneak into the backyard. If it was one of the kids, she'd slap them hard on the back with a broomstick. If one of the young mothers went out back to pick up a fallen piece of laundry, the Witch would scream something incomprehensible at them and scare them away.

I don't know who started it, but there was a rumor among the kids that the backyard had an herb garden that the Witch cultivated in order to make all sorts of poisons—and that the garden was guarded by a tiger. I still remember how every spring, night after night, I could hear the strangest animal noises.

"Then there's the other side of it. Why can't anybody just mind their own business? It's not like they actually care about you or anything, but they're still happy to tell you that what you're doing isn't right when they should really just stay out of it. They're so annoying, and I'm so alone—I feel like I might forget who I am."

When I was in second grade or so, I hatched a plan to get into the Witch's garden. None of the children had managed to see it, and I wanted to use it as my personal playground. So early one Saturday morning, I set my plan into action. I knew the Witch would drag herself down the stairs in the afternoon to do her usual weeding. And on Saturdays, my parents always slept in until about nine. I assumed that as long as I locked the door quietly when I left, I'd be able to sneak out unnoticed. Before I left, I grabbed my key and removed my teddy bear keychain. The bear had a tiny bell around its neck—and the last thing I wanted to do was wake the tiger.

It was May, and it was a little hot, a little humid. Still, today was going to be the day. I woke up naturally, probably because I was nervous. I wasn't tired at all, and without opening the curtains I could tell that night was almost over. I put my hand over my pounding heart—it was almost as if I had a small bird inside of me—then headed down the apartment stairs.

". . . And that's why I'm going to keep the lie."

"Keep the lie?"

Hosono's big eyes were shining. I was sure of it now. She was the one I'd seen here early in the winter. She was wearing a red down jacket—undeniably carrying the real thing inside of her.

"Even if it's a lie, it's a place of my own. That's why I'm going to keep it. It doesn't need to be a big lie—just big enough for one person. And if I can hold on to that lie inside my heart, if I can keep repeating it to myself, it might lead me somewhere. Somewhere else, somewhere different. If I can do that, maybe I'll change a little, and maybe the world will, too."

In the garden, I found no tiger. No herbs, either. There was only color—it was filled with so much color.

Roses, spirea, peonies, lilies of the valley, prairie gentians, and so many other flowers that I couldn't name. As the dark sky packed with midnight's secrets started to give way to the beginnings of light, I saw every color blooming around me, laughing joyously. The flowers were dressed up in pearls of morning dew, their ephemeral perfume tickling the inside of my brain.

I found myself looking at my hands. I simply couldn't believe I'd been allowed to witness this spectacle without leaving my own body. The wildflowers swayed elegantly to a waltz that nobody could hear, clinging dearly to the final dance of the night. Every petal gave off a glow of its own as it released the moonlight absorbed throughout the night. The flowers were beckoning me.

I wanted to touch them with my own hands.

I got on my tiptoes and reached out for the sweetly

drooping wisteria. It looked so soft. Beyond my fingers, just beyond my reach, there was a crack. The morning sun. Dawn was breaking. The spell was broken, the colors around me changing with dizzying speed. Before I could even blink, the small world around me had become immersed in morning.

Then I saw her. The Witch was under a wisteria trellis. She was putting out milk for all the kittens gathered around her feet. I saw her hunch her bulky shoulders in annoyance as she noticed the color of the sky. Once she had put away the bottle of milk, she walked off, the kittens purring softly as they followed after her. As soon as the Witch and her kittens were out of sight, the sky took on a familiar face. It was morning. I didn't make a sound. I stood there frozen for a couple of moments, then went home the same way I had come.

When I opened the front door, my mom was waiting for me. She said she'd gotten up to go to the bathroom and saw my door open. Then she found the teddy bear. Where were you? she asked angrily. I was sure she was going to wake up my dad. My mom's questions kept me on my toes, but I could barely keep myself from collapsing right there. When my mom gave up on the interrogation and let me go, I crawled into bed. At the edge of sleep, I remembered.

How the scene of the Witch and her kittens—blessed by the wisteria—somehow looked like a painting I'd once seen of the Virgin.

Hosono wasn't rocking anymore. Just standing there, under the streetlamp. Yuri was breathing softly.

That one's me, Hosono said as she pointed at her building. It was a new complex that couldn't have been more than a couple of years old. Must be expensive, I thought, looking at the sofa in the lobby. I'd noticed it the last time I'd walked by. The lights were still on in one room on the fifth floor. "Can you make it home?" I asked. Hosono gave a little nod. As she stroked Yuri's round head with her left hand, her wedding band gleamed in the light of the lamp.

"Sheeba . . ."

We'd already said goodbye and I was about to walk home when Hosono called my name.

"Are you lying about something?"

"Mhm," I said, then waved goodbye. Hosono waved back.

I stroked my belly as I went down the hill. It was a little calmer now than when I'd left my apartment. I used the flashlight on my phone to guide the way, occasionally resting a hand on the wall beside me. When I reached the bottom of the hill, I looked south. There it was again: the red star. Still blinking, moving slowly through the sky.

The first thing I need to do when I get home is turn on the light.

WEEK 38

My baby dropped a little lower right before Golden Week. According to Baby-N-Me, this wasn't anything to worry about. It just meant the baby was on its way. It was harder for me to move around now, but it was actually easier to breathe. The kicking wasn't bothering me so much anymore, my appetite had returned, and I was even sleeping better.

I opened the browser on my phone and searched for "walking late in pregnancy."

Every time I visit the doctor, he shows me my baby on the screen. He's gotten clearer with every visit. Last time, he was actually posing for us, making a peace sign. I couldn't believe it. This baby of mine has to be some kind of genius.

Aerobics has been as grueling as ever. Every time I go, I wonder if it's going to be the death of me. And here I thought childbirth was going to do me in. Anyway, I haven't given up yet. The woman in the neon-blue shirt isn't coming anymore. I hope she had a safe delivery. I really do.

When I was changing one day, Curly gave me some body cream with a really nice scent. She's heading to her parents' this weekend so she can have the baby back home.

"Let me know when you give birth. You're having your baby here, right? I'll be back soon. By the way, I've been meaning to ask you about your phone case.... Did you get that from one of their shows? I like them, too. Once everything's settled down, we should go see them together. We can ask our husbands to look after the kids."

"Yeah, that'd be amazing. Let's do it!"

I figured the city would be crowded over the holidays, so I spent most of my time at home. I'd already seen every movie I wanted to see in theaters and been to all the good exhibits at the museums. In an otherwise silent museum on a weekday, I'd heard two women talking in front of a Van Gogh. "These colors are incredible, don't you think?" "I know, what a genius . . ." I wanted to pass on their words to the artist himself—the artist who had sold only one painting in his lifetime. On my way out, I bought a sunflower tea towel from the gift shop. That was the day before the holidays started.

The stretch of amazing weather continued, one day after another. The sky was so blue that I saw it even with my eyes closed. Early summer was buzzing inside me, making me feel like I was on vacation even though I was just staying at home. I didn't go anywhere special, but I stopped by the gelato place by the river every day. I'd go out for a walk, buy some gelato on my way home, then pull a chair out to the balcony and eat it there. I'd stretch out in my T-shirt, shorts, and sunglasses, closing my eyes and rubbing my belly. I almost felt as if I'd come to some sort of resort town in Italy, even though I'd never been anywhere like that. "Feel that sun. This is the life, huh?"

I felt my belly move in response.

On the last day of the holidays, Momoi sent me a text in the morning, and Yukino called me around 6:00 p.m. One of our former coworkers who had gotten married and built a new home was having a housewarming party next month. "What do you think? Wanna go?" Yukino asked. "I'm a little busy," I told her. "I'd better pass." Once we'd talked about a few other things and I was about ready to go, Yukino said, "Oh, by the way, I got divorced," then acted like she was about to hang up. Shocked, I asked her to tell me about it. . . . Typical Yukino. It's just like her to move ahead with things without anyone even catching on. But it's probably like that for everybody. Yukino's more open than most, maybe. She's a good egg.

That night, I turned out the light and got into bed, but I couldn't get to sleep. Random thoughts flashed in the darkness, then vanished: the voice of the DJ on the radio when I was making dinner, the band posters on my wall, the way this coworker I've almost never talked to was always biting his nails. I drifted there, wherever I was, in a space that was full of everything but had no sound, no time, no up, no down.

I turned the light back on.

I almost forgot. I squinted at the pale blue light of my phone as I opened Baby-N-Me and wrote down what had happened that day: what I'd eaten, how much I'd exercised, how the baby was doing. Words summoned more words. When I was done, I pressed the SAVE icon and a notification popped up:

CONGRATULATIONS! YOU'VE USED BABY-N-ME 100 DAYS IN A ROW. Now satisfied, I turned the light off again. This time, sleep made its way through my apartment walls and came to carry me away. Back once more—somewhere between dream and reality.

○—————————○

The ABCs of Real Estate, Real Estate Exam Prep: Cracking the Civil Code. Giant text, pink and blue figures. Why do books like these always have geometric patterns on their covers? Figures that don't actually exist anywhere. I open one of the books with a snap, its pages breaking loose from their gluey confinement. So textbooks are the same as they were when I was a student, right down to that new-paper smell.

The textbook I had out on my kilim was so intimidating, but full of promise at the same time. Opening these books as an adult, I couldn't shake this feeling—like they just might help me get away from where I was now.

As I turned off the TV, the baby kicked in apparent protest. I said back in a firm voice:

"Hey, it's time for Mommy to do a little studying."

Four days early. It was still dark out, and I'd just been ripped from the middle of a dream. It didn't take long for me to realize that something was happening inside me. As I lay there, I felt an occasional pain like menstrual cramps, but the pain soon started growing intense and more frequent. I checked my underwear, and it looked like I was bleeding. All of this was new to me, like nothing I'd ever experienced before.

In a cold sweat, completely unable to speak, I called to her in my mind—not as a believer, but as a peer.

Mary. Dear Mary. I have to say it. I have no idea how you did it. I can't even imagine what you were going through, having a baby with only a carpenter for a husband and a pony or something. I know the angels and the wise men showed up after that, but I'm pretty sure you would have preferred a nurse or an ob-gyn, right? Wait, did you have those back then? God, it must have been really cold, though. A December birth? Well, I don't know. Maybe December is actually pretty hot in Palestine. Sorry, I really should know more about you.

Anyway, it's May in Japan. That's going to be a big help when I'm looking for daycare. These days, lots of women want to keep working after they have children—sometimes they need to—and they don't have anywhere to put them. It's kind of a big deal. They're always talking about it on the news. It was March when Chiharu had her twins, and in Japan the school year starts in April, so she had a really hard time finding a place for her girls. Sounds terrible, right? Having a baby isn't easy. Damned if you do, damned if you don't. It's been two thousand years, and it's the same old story, right? Anyway, you should come and visit sometime.

I actually looked into daycare. Into a few different programs and different kinds of support. I'm doing a little better than last time, right? I guess I figured I might as well make the most of my situation. Even if it is just a lie. The world's what we make it, right? Even if it's just us, on our own—with the whole world against us.

I get out of bed, then put on my socks.

TWELVE MONTHS LATER

At work, everybody had learned how to make the coffee—with the sole exception of the section head.

"We've got green tea, too," Higashinakano said, looking pleased as he showed me the selection.

I was sure it was going to be tea bags, but to my surprise they were using an actual teapot. They apparently bought the leaves in bulk from Lohaco.

Maternity leave was over. I came back to work to find my old section different—just a little different. If the phone rang four times or so, somebody would pick up. When the mail and faxes started piling up, the first person to notice would make sure it got taken care of. When the copier ran out of ink, the person who was using the machine would replace the cartridge without pretending they hadn't noticed. If anyone saw something on the floor, they'd pick it up. When we got boxes of sweets from clients, it was no longer one person's job to go around the office doling them out. There was a desk called the snack station, and everyone could go there to collect their own treats. Today, Tanaka cut the baumkuchen.

"Sorato's a real cutie pie, isn't he?"

Higashinakano was grinning like crazy as he handed my phone back to me.

I'm following a mom on Instagram who had a boy last May, right when I had Sorato. I save all the photos and videos she posts, then show them to people when they ask to see my baby. Thanks to her, Sorato keeps getting bigger all the time. The other day, he learned how to pull himself up. He has a stuffed sea lion that makes noise when you shake it, and he loves the thing to death, but he loves music more than anything. You should see him shake his little tush every time he hears his favorite song.

Even if that mom on Instagram gets flamed, I hope she keeps going—at least until the people around me lose interest in Sorato.

"This is a great place to work if you have a child. You won't have any problem taking time off when you need it, and everybody's supportive if you have to leave work early because your baby has a fever. You know how babies are always getting fevers."

"Oh, it happens all the time, trust me. To be honest, I wish I could count on my husband to take care of some things, but at least my parents live close by. That's a huge help. And, ladies, I'm telling you this for your own good, but make sure you find a guy who's willing to help out!"

As quiet laughter filled the tiny event space, the two women from HR looked around the room with satisfied expressions on their faces.

I'm at a job fair today. This panel, "Balancing Your Career and Your Life," is offered specifically to women, as if work-life balance is something only women need to consider. They asked employees (age twenty-five to forty-four) from several sections who had taken maternity leave to come forward and speak—and that included me. One of the HR women held the mic up and started to talk.

"Now let's hear from Shibata-san. She had a baby last year and just came back to work this month. Care to share your thoughts?"

Under her perfectly curved bangs, she shot me a look telling me it was my turn. She had dimples like a chipmunk. This was my first time working with her. She'd apparently joined the company while I was on leave. Her cream-colored suit looked ridiculously expensive. I guess she really wanted to look her best for the event. I switched on my mic.

"That's right, I just got back. I agree. I think this is a great place to work. Everyone in my section has been really helpful. Thanks to them, I can leave a little after five to pick up my son from daycare."

"That's wonderful to hear. And has your work changed at all since coming back? Also, does your family help? Can you tell us a little about your professional goals going forward?"

I took a moment to think, then lifted the mic.

"My work . . . Well, nothing's really changed in terms of my actual responsibilities since I had my baby. It's the little things: serving tea, cleaning out the fridge. I don't do much of that anymore. It's made it a lot easier to focus on my actual work. I'm not married, so I don't have a husband. And I still haven't told my parents about the baby. Fortunately, Sorato's been a real angel, so I haven't had any issues. He doesn't even cry at night. And professional goals . . . Well, at the moment, I'm looking into changing jobs. I've been studying for the real estate exam."

The older emcee panicked and asked another panelist to talk. Meanwhile, one seat over, the chipmunk's dimples had vanished. I wondered if I'd gone too far. Should I apologize after? But for what?

As I listened to the others talk, I looked out at the faces in the audience: women in their early twenties, all of them in suits. How many of them were there? I could see they were driven, and passionate about their future careers, but were they considering having babies of their own, too?

Yeah, I'd love to have another baby. Maybe by the time I'm thirty-seven.